Robert

Jeanette
Great to meet
you!
Tracie x

By: Tracie Podger

Copyright

Robert

ISBN-13: 978-1501071218

ISBN-10: 1501071211

About the Author

Tracie Podger currently lives in Kent, UK with her husband and a rather obnoxious cat called George. She's a Padi Scuba Diving Instructor with a passion for writing. Tracie has been fortunate to have dived some of the wonderful oceans of the world where she can indulge in another hobby, underwater photography. She likes getting up close and personal with sharks.

Tracie wishes to thank you for giving your time to read her books and hopes you enjoy them as much as she loves writing them. If you would like to know more, please feel free to contact her, she would love to hear from you.

Publicist, Paula Radell, can be contacted via
Passionatepromos@gmail.com

Twitter: @Tracie Podger

Facebook: Tracie Podger, Author

www.TraciePodger.com

Available in ebook and paperback....

Fallen Angel, Part I

Fallen Angel, Part II

Evelyn - A novella to accompany the Fallen Angel Series

Robert - A prequel to Fallen Angel, Part I

Coming soon....

Fallen Angel, Part III
Fallen Angel, Part IV
A Virtual Affair
The Passion Series

Acknowledgements

I could never have written the Fallen Angel series without the support of my family. My husband has been my rock, without him, I wouldn't be here.

My heartfelt thanks to the best readers and proofreaders a girl could want, Romy Lazzari, Janet Hughes and Paula Radell. Your input is invaluable.

Thank you to Margreet Asslebergs of Rebel Edit & Design for the wonderful cover.

And last but certainly not least, a big hug to my publicist and friend, Paula Radell. She is one of the kindest people I've come across on this journey called self publishing. Paula is responsible for getting my books out there and I am overwhelmed by her support and belief in The Fallen Angel Series.

Paula Radell - Passionate Promotions

So how did this all start? It's been a long journey but my love of writing came about after I was encouraged to do so as part of my recovery from depression. I have always loved to read and lose myself in books, words soothe me.

One day, after a series of dreams, I sat with my laptop and the words flowed from my fingertips - pages and pages of them. I forgot my troubles and lost myself in the characters I have created. I hope you can too.

No matter what people tell you, words and ideas can change the world - Robin Williams

Contents

Chapter One

The house was empty when I arrived home from school. I fished out the key attached by a piece of string to the inside of my blazer pocket. I wasn't surprised to find myself alone, it was quite normal. I shrugged off my blazer and unclipped the red striped tie we were made to wear, hanging them neatly on the banister. I made my way to the kitchen, dropped my bag on the floor and opened the fridge. There was a piece of cheese as hard as a brick, a half empty tin of beans and a carton of milk. I sniffed the milk. I had learnt over the years that if it had a certain smell it wouldn't taste nice. It seemed fine so I poured it over some slightly soft cereal in a bowl. I switched on the TV and waited. They never came home.

I must have fallen asleep on the sofa and it was dark outside when I was awoken by a knock at the front door. The room was illuminated only by the flickering screen of the TV. I waited until there was a second knock before I made my way to the hall. I wasn't normally allowed to open the door, but maybe it was them. Maybe they had forgotten their door key.

I looked through the letter box, someone outside bent down so their eyes were level with mine.

"Hello son, can you open the door for us?" he asked.

He looked like a policeman, I had seen them before. They came to my school sometimes and of course I had seen them on the TV.

"My mum says I'm not allowed to open the door, to anyone," I said.

"Is there an adult with you? Can they open the door?" he asked.

"No," I replied, quietly.

I watched the man stand up, speak to someone behind him before crouching back down again.

"It's okay son, we just need to come in and make sure you're all right," he said.

"I had my tea," I replied. "I made it myself."

"Well, that's good, what did you have?"

"Cornflakes," I said. "I like cornflakes."

"I like cornflakes too," he replied. "Did you have lots of milk?"

That was silly, of course I had lots of milk, everyone has lots of milk with cornflakes, don't they? He stood again and then I saw Nora from next door, she placed her hand on the letterbox, her old creaky legs bent down so she could see through.

"Robert, can you open the door, love," she said.

I liked Nora, she gave me sweets sometimes. She would be in the garden pegging out her washing and she would see me peering over the fence at her. Smiling, she would raise her fingers to her lips, creep back into her house and come out with a packet of boiled sweets. Sometimes they were so sticky I couldn't get the wrapper off. I wasn't allowed sweets normally, bad for your teeth and full of animal stuff, my mum used to tell me.

I opened the door and outside, standing under the little porch light was Nora and the policeman, there was another coming up the path, a police lady. I stood, blocking the way.

"Can we come in son?" the man asked.

At school my teacher had told me that we should always listen and be polite to the police so I let them pass and followed into the lounge. Nora crouched down to my level.

"Robert, is there anyone here with you?" she asked.

"No, I'm waiting for my mum and dad. They're normally home by now," I said, shaking a little.

Something was wrong, I could sense it. I had seen the look that passed between the police and Nora just before she ushered me to the sofa and sat next to me. She took my hand in hers and it felt odd. I don't think anyone had held my hand before. My mum pulled me across the road sometimes by it, if I wasn't quick enough. I looked at my hand in hers. She had funny, bent fingers and long, yellowing nails. It looked like she had been gardening again, she had dirty fingertips.

"Robert, have you got any aunties, someone who lives nearby?" she asked.

I shook my head, I didn't think so. My mum would talk on the phone to people but no one ever visited us. Unless my dad was around, she never really left the house either.

"What about nanny, where does she live?" she asked.

I thought for a minute. "I don't think I have one of them."

"Son, how old are you?" the man asked.

"Six, I will be seven in two months and twenty-eight days," I replied, proudly. I was good at math.

"Your mum didn't leave anyone here to look after you?" he asked.

"No, I come home from school and sometimes they're out so I make my own tea. I have reading to do, I can read well now."

I picked up my school book to show them. It was one I had selected from the bookshelf in my class about football, but they didn't seem interested. Nora stood, they huddled together whispering and I watched them, trying real hard to hear what was being said.

"Where's my mum?" I asked, hating that my voice quivered a little.

I was trying to be strong, that's what my mum would have wanted. She hated it if I cried, she would want me to be strong. "Be a man," she would say. I tried to be a man.

"I have some terrible news, Robert," Nora said to me as she sat back down. "Your mum and dad, well, there's been an accident, in the car."

"Are they in the hospital?" I asked.

"Well, yes they are, but..."

"Can I go and see them?" I interrupted.

"Robert, the thing is, no you can't see them. Oh love, they..., they've gone to heaven," Nora blurted out, her face screwed up in sadness.

"Heaven," the voice in my head said. "I doubt that very much."

I didn't have voices in my head all the time, not like mad people got. Just every now and again a voice would warn me of something, like to look further up the road and when I did there would be a bike coming that I hadn't noticed before. My mum said I have good instinct. I didn't know what that meant, but right then I hoped it was a good thing.

The policeman and Nora were chatting, the police lady came and sat on the other side of me, she seemed friendly and she smiled at me.

"Do you have any friends, Robert, maybe someone you stayed overnight with?" she asked.

I shook my head, my mum didn't really like me to have friends. I was never allowed to bring anyone home and I hadn't been invited to stay overnight with anyone.

"No aunties, uncles?"

"My dad used to speak to someone, she lives in a different country. I think it was his sister," I volunteered. "I answered the phone once, she said Happy Easter to me."

"Do you know her name or maybe she had an accent, did she sound funny?" she asked.

"Yes, my teacher has the same voice," I replied, excited. "He comes from America. I saw America on a map once, shall I show it to you?"

I had a map book in my bedroom. My dad used to sit on my bed and talk about all the different countries. He would make up a story about a little boy who would travel the world. I knew it was made up because he called the little boy Robert and I hadn't been anywhere. Running up the stairs, I pulled down the book from the shelf above my bed.

I showed the policeman the book, smiling because I found America straight away. He patted me on the head before he made his way to the front door speaking on the black thing he had attached to his jacket.

****

That night I stayed with Nora, she had a little back bedroom, same as mine and she tucked me into bed. Sitting on the edge, she watched me and stroked my black hair away from my forehead.

"So, if they have gone to heaven, does that mean they're not coming back?" I asked.

"Oh love, no, they're not coming back," she said.

"Where am I going to live?"

"Let's worry about that tomorrow, shall we?" she replied.

She sat with me for a while. She didn't have to I thought, but it was nice to have someone stroke my hair. As I lay in the dark I thought about my mum and dad and what Nora had told me. Maybe I should be crying but however much I screwed my eyes shut, the tears wouldn't come. I pinched myself on the arm, hard enough to bruise, but that didn't make me cry either. I felt something strange in my belly though, like a pain but not a pain. It was like my belly was empty. Maybe I just needed something to eat.

Downstairs Nora met with the police again and this time someone new, I could hear them chatting. I heard the word Social Services but I didn't know what that meant. I crept to the top of the stairs and listened. They were saying that I would stay with Nora until emergency foster parents could be found in the morning. I would have liked to have stayed at home, I was okay on my own. I knew how to make my tea, I did it all the time and I didn't want to miss school. I liked school.

The following morning a new lady came, she said her name was Sarah and she was going to take me to her house to stay for a while. She told me about the toys she had there, that I could play with. She was an older woman but she had kind eyes. I liked people's eyes, it told me a lot about them. I could always tell if someone was friendly or not by their eyes. My mum asked me about it once. She wanted to know how I knew what people were like just by looking at them. I couldn't answer the question though, I thought everybody could see what I saw. I got told off a lot for staring though.

"Are you ready?" Sarah asked as we stood in the sitting room.

"I think so. Can I get my teddy?" I asked.

She looked at Nora. "Do you have a key?" she asked.

"I don't, maybe the police do," Nora answered.

Sarah bent down to my level, she looked straight at me with a smile.

"How about I get in touch with someone later and we can ask," she said.

She took me in a car; I sat in the back and we drove, not very far, until we pulled into her driveway. She had a small house in a little lane with fields either side and a dog. It came bounding to the door when she opened it. It was only little but licked my face when I bent down to stroke its rough brown fur. I liked her dog, she told me he was called Benny. Benny and me became friends, we played in the garden and I stayed at Sarah's house for a few weeks.

****

I liked the house, it was bigger than mine and there were lots of windows. At home my mum used to pull the curtains closed all the time, making the rooms dark, but at Sarah's it was always light. I had a bedroom to myself, there were no other children but some must have lived there before because there were so many boxes of toys and not just for boys either. I found a box of dolls which I put straight back under the bed.

"Sarah, there are dolls under the bed," I told her.

"I know, I don't suppose you want to play with them. Would you like me to put them somewhere else?" she replied.

"No, it's okay, I just wanted you to know."

"Your tea will be ready soon, do you want to go and wash your hands?" she said.

One of the best things was that Sarah cooked proper food. I found it strange to sit at a dining table and eat with a knife and fork, I had forgotten how to use them. At school I had sandwiches for lunch and at home we usually ate something in a bowl with a spoon. It was at tea time that Sarah and me talked. We would talk about all sorts of things, school, my mum and dad and sometimes she asked me how I felt but I didn't know the words, so I said nothing about that. At night she would tuck me in bed and sit with me, either to read or just to put her arm around my shoulders. My mum wasn't a huggy person so it was good to snuggle up to Sarah sometimes, not always, but just sometimes when I was scared. She always smelled lovely and I liked to bury my head in her shoulder and listen to her voice as she read to me. She read me a book about another little boy who had lost his mum and dad. But this little boy used to cry and I wondered why I didn't. Then I would remember, I was being a man and men don't cry - I know that because my mum told me, men don't cry.

I did go back to school after a couple of days and people were different to me. The teachers were a bit kinder. Not that they were horrible in the first place but the kids were strange around me, as if they didn't want to be friends anymore. It was not like I had many friends at school. I was more interested in learning new things than chatting, but at playtime I might be invited to play football or climb on the frame. They didn't ask me anymore, but I saw them whisper about me, behind their hands, their eyes looking my way. I wanted to ask them what they were talking about but I never did, I just sat on my own until playtime was over.

****

One day I was taken to the Head Masters office, there was a man there that I didn't know and I hoped I was not in trouble. I was asked to sit down as the man wanted to have a chat to me.

"Hello, Robert, my name is David, I'm a doctor," he said.

"Hello," I replied. I wasn't sick, well, I didn't think I was.

"I thought it might be good to have a chat, maybe about your mum and dad."

"Oh, okay," I replied.

"Do you want to talk about them?" he asked.

Did I? Sarah asked me many questions about them and I didn't mind talking to her but I didn't know this man and my mum told me not to talk to strangers.

"Not really," I said.

He asked me if I felt sad about them dying. What a dumb question, of course I was sad. They were dead. I didn't answer so he asked me if I liked being at Sarah's house.

"I like Benny," I said. "Sarah is nice, she cooks real food you know. She made me, oh what was it called, spaghetti something last night. I've never had that before, I think it comes from abroad. We got real messy when we ate, it was fun."

"Did your mum ever cook?" he asked.

I shook my head. No, my mum rarely cooked, we lived on whatever could be opened and eaten straight away. Sometimes there was no real food in the house so we just had toast or cereal. I had heard my dad shout at her once, about making sure I had a proper meal each night but it never happened. I had my main meal at school, at lunchtimes. It was usually a little packed lunch that came in a bag, a sandwich and a piece of fruit. If the dinner lady was feeling really kind, she would give me a bar of chocolate.

"What about your dad?" he asked. "Do you want to talk about him?"

"My dad didn't live with us all the time," I said.

Sometimes he would, he would stay for a few days but then got the calling, as my mum would put it. He wanted to be an artist, he used to draw pictures of me and I had them pinned to the wall in my bedroom. Sometimes he had to go, sort his head out, I was told. I guessed everyone's dad did that. I missed him when he was gone. My mum was always sad then. Sometimes she would shout and scream about his other family, I didn't know what she meant. She would point to me and tell me I had made him go away and that he didn't love us enough to stay.

It was at times like that I did what I knew made her happy. I poured the brown stuff from the bottle under the sink and she would cry while she drank lots of it. After a while she would fall asleep on the sofa and I would cover her over with a blanket. She would still be there in the morning, looking really strange. She would have little lines of black paint running down her cheeks from her eyelashes. I would try to rub it away with my fingers sometimes, to make her pretty again. I hated the smell of the brown stuff. One day I had tasted it. It was like drinking fire, it burnt my mouth and my throat. It made me cough and my eyes watered.

"Do you think your mum loved you?" he asked, now this startled me.

After thinking for a moment, I answered.

"No," I said with clarity.

I knew she didn't love me, I think she liked me though, I was no trouble. I kept myself to myself and stayed in my bedroom most of the time. I did what I was told, I didn't cry and whine like other kids. I dressed and cleaned my teeth without being asked every morning. I took myself off to school when the big hand on the clock said so and I brought myself home straight after. She never hit me, ever.

"Why do you think your mum didn't love you?" he asked.

I didn't answer. When it was home time, other kids had mums that hugged them and laughed and asked them how their day had been. I watched kids show their mum a drawing or a book. Mine never did that and if I showed her a book she would swipe her arm, knocking it to the floor. She told me not to fill my head with rubbish. I didn't know how to fill my head with rubbish but I liked reading my books. If she loved me, she would laugh and be happy, wouldn't she?

Session over, I went back to my class with no real understanding of what that was all about.

So it went on, people asking me questions about my parents and how did I feel about it? Throughout the whole time I had not shed one tear. I didn't think they would understand what was going on in my head, so I said very little. I didn't like them keep asking questions, especially when I did answer them. I started to get angry.

"Did your mum ever hit you?"

"No."

"Did your mum ever hug you?"

"No."

"Did your mum play with you?"

"No."

"Did your dad play with you?"

"Sometimes."

I saw the way their eyes shifted, the way their eyebrows went up when I answered. I was not stupid, they didn't like my mum or maybe they didn't believe me. The more they asked, the more confused and quieter I became. The stiller I was, the more nervous they became, they seemed uncomfortable around me. I felt it, I saw it in their eyes.

****

A few weeks had passed and after returning from school one day, I met an elderly woman. Apparently she was my aunt Edith, my dad's sister and the person I had spoken to on the phone that one time. She looked so different to me. She had grey hair, pulled back in a tight bun and runny, grey eyes with fair, leathery skin. Then again, my mum and dad looked different too. I had black hair and dark, dark eyes. Sometimes I would look in the mirror and I couldn't decide if they were brown or black. My mum was blonde with light hazel eyes and as much as I tried, I couldn't quite remember what colour my dad's eyes were. I got upset when I couldn't remember the colour, I didn't want to forget him.

"Robert, this is Edith, she's your aunt and she's come from America to visit you," Sarah said.

"Hello, Robert, I'm pleased to finally meet you," Edith replied, holding out her hand for me to shake.

I wasn't sure what to do, but I shook it anyway.

"Hello," I replied.

"I'm sorry to hear about your mum and dad. I've been asked to take you home with me for a while," she said.

I didn't want to go, I was happy at Sarah's but what I didn't like the most was that she didn't have kind eyes. She never looked at me, she never let me look at her. If I tried to move my head, to look at her face, she would turn away slightly. It confused me.

"Thank you but I don't want to," I replied.

"I have a house with a woods and guess what? Some deer come and feed in the garden," Edith said.

Deer? That made me smile. I had never seen a real one before.

"Wow, that sounds cool," I said, getting a little excited.

Sarah sat beside me and sometimes I caught them looking at each other, over my head. Sarah would nod and smile at Edith but her smile didn't seem right. It wasn't the same smile she would give me. The smile that made the skin around her eyes crinkle. She didn't like Edith, I thought, and I wondered why. You see, if the skin around the eyes crinkled it was a good smile, a friendly one. If it didn't, then I knew it wasn't good. That was one of the reasons I liked to look at people's eyes.

"There's a school nearby you can go to, but you have get a bus. It will pick you up at the top of the lane every morning. I spoke with the school, they are looking forward to meeting you," Edith said.

"Oh, what about my own school?" I asked.

"They won't mind, as long as you go to school it doesn't matter which one it is, does it Sarah," she replied.

Sarah never answered but kept that strange half smile on her face. Edith was to collect me a couple of days later I was told. After she had left Sarah and me sat in the sitting room. She seemed a bit sad and I took her hand.

"It's okay, Sarah. I won't be gone long and we can take Benny to the park when I get back," I said.

She smiled sadly at me, patted my hand and went to make dinner. I did notice she had tears in her eyes though.

I wanted to go back to my old house to collect some things. Driving past it one day, on the way to school, I had noticed a sign outside, it had been put up for sale. I didn't know who was dealing with that, I guess my aunt would, but then, what did I know about these things. It seemed my aunt thought that the best thing was to forget about my parents as soon as possible. She never mentioned them and I knew that she hadn't seen her brother for many years. We have lived in the same house all my life and she had never visited. She only ever rang at Easter and Christmas to speak to my dad. Not that he was there every Christmas. When he wasn't I didn't get a present, we didn't have a cooked meal or laugh and have fun. It was just a normal day.

She had told me we were going on a plane to America. At first I had thought it was a holiday, I would be back. I didn't have time to say goodbye to anyone, I would have liked to have said goodbye to my teacher at least. I would've also liked to have taken some of my own clothes with me and my teddy, the one present my mum ever gave me, but no. We simply got into a car and was driven to the airport. I didn't understand why Sarah was so upset when we climbed into that car, she tried to smile but as she hugged me to her I heard a little sob.

I was excited though, I'd never been on a plane before and with my nose pressed to the window in the departure lounge, I watched them take off and arrive. I bounced around in excitement, wanting to get on that plane quickly, to have an adventure.

The journey was long. I had a window seat and I watched the ground fall away, the clouds disperse as we flew through them until all that was above us was miles and miles of sky. As the night fell, I looked at the stars, so bright and clear. If heaven was above me, then I wondered, if I looked hard enough, could I see my mum and dad? Were they one of the stars that twinkled down at me? Nora had said they had gone to heaven and as she was so old, she must know these things.

I had fallen asleep and was woken by a jolt as the plane landed. The captain announced our arrival in Pittsburgh and after a little while we made our way through the airport. We had no luggage to collect and soon enough we were outside in the sun. The heat was quite something. I had to shield my eyes from the glare of the sun as it reflected off the cars, off the buildings. It smelt different too, the air I mean.

It felt like a long journey in a cab until eventually we reached the town of Sterling. I read the little sign as a few buildings came into view. It was rural with wooden houses dotted around, the complete opposite to where I had lived in a little terrace house in the South East of London. Everyone had a big car, a truck Edith had called them. Some were broken and one we had passed had no wheels. It didn't look very tidy, people had really long grass in the front garden but every now and again, I would spot a kid, playing. They would stop and look at my face pressed to the car window as we passed.

Pulling up at my aunt's house was an eye opener. There were indeed acres of garden and the house was surrounded by woodland. It was one storey but with a basement and a wooden porch wrapping around it. The paint was peeling off the wood and I had to be careful not to tread on the rotted planks. There was a swing seat on the porch and I wanted to sit and throw my legs back and forth to make it rock. I bet it even made a creaking sound too.

Aunt Edith showed me to my new bedroom. It was okay, it had a small metal bed under the one window with a patchwork quilt thrown over it. There was a book shelf, I liked to read, but making my way over to it, I noticed all it held were bibles, all sorts. Some had pictures, some just words. I had seen bibles in school, we had started to learn about the different Gods. There were no colouring books though and I wanted to practice my colouring. I was getting good at keeping the pen inside the lines.

A small wooden wardrobe, which held a collection of clothes for me and a desk with a metal chair were the only other things in the room. No toys, no TV, no books or colouring pens, no teddies, none of the things I had got used to having at Sarah's. There was nothing from my old home, none of the pictures I had on the wall that my dad had drawn. The walls were just bare, painted a sickly yellow colour and there were no curtains at the window. I climbed on the bed to look out the window, all I could see were trees and more trees.

"Do you like your room?" Edith asked. "I got some clothes from the Church, you'll need to thank them. I'm sure they will fit okay."

"Erm, yes, it's nice," I replied. I wasn't sure what she would say if I said no.

"Well, feel free to have a look around," she said, as she made her way out of the room.

While Edith unpacked her small case in the second bedroom, I investigated the rest of the house. I found a kitchen with a wooden, scrubbed table in the middle and mismatched chairs tucked in around it, a lounge with an open fireplace and a couple of battered sofas facing it. In one corner there was a desk with yet more bibles stacked on top and through the kitchen, I found two doors. One led to the bathroom and one to a basement. Down a flight of stairs, I noticed some kind of workbench and stacks and stacks of logs for the fire were drying out. There were piles of old newspapers and tins of paint but that was all.

****

For the first couple of days I was allowed to explore a little, to find my way through the woods and back to the house. I made a plan of camps I could make in there, playing soldiers. Then, on the third day, dressed in shorts and a blue button down shirt, I was sent to school. I had a sandwich and an apple in my back pack and Edith waited at the end of the lane for the bus to arrive. I wasn't scared about going to school on my own, I did it all the time but what bothered me was, if I was on holiday, why did I need to go to school at all?

My mum took me out of school all the time. Sometimes we would drive for long hours to meet my dad who had holed himself up in a beach shack somewhere, to paint. I had not had to go to school though, this was something new.

I climbed aboard the bus, it was nearly full but the kids quietened when I got on so I took the first seat available, next to a girl. She smiled at me. She reminded me a little of my mum, she had blond hair in pigtails and kind, hazel eyes. The first thing I noticed were the bruises on her skinny, bare arms.

"Hi, my name's Cara, what's yours?"

"Robert," was all I said, shyly.

"You speak funny," she said, but I didn't think she was being unkind.

"Well, so do you. I come from England," I replied.

"Where's that?"

I shrugged my shoulders. "I had to get on a plane so it must have been far away."

"I've never been on a plane before," she said.

"It was cool, really fast and we went really high in the sky. I could see the stars and everything," I gushed.

"You saw the stars? I love looking at the stars, they're so pretty," she said excitedly.

We arrived at the school, there was a woman waiting to meet us and I was escorted off the bus with Cara in tow and led to a classroom. I was introduced to my new teacher, Father Peters and I didn't like him, he didn't have friendly eyes at all. I sat next to Cara that day, she showed me where we went to eat our lunch and she was kind to me. My first ever friend, I thought. The school was small, attached to the church and when it was play time there were no swings, no climbing frame, none of the things I had back home. Cara and I sat on the dried up grass and just chatted.

"Where do you live?" I asked.

"Not too far, we have a farm."

"That's cool, do you have animals?"

"Yes, I have to get up early and feed the chickens every day, they run around the yard and sometimes get in the house," she said, with a laugh.

"Can I come and see them one day?" I asked.

"Erm, well, my dad is not real friendly. I don't think he would like that," she replied.

"Oh, is your mum friendly?" I asked.

"Yes, when she's not sad."

"My mum was always sad, she's dead you know. So is my dad."

"Oh, that's real terrible. Who do you live with?"

"My aunt, her name is Edith. Do you have any brothers?" I asked.

"I had a sister but she doesn't live with us anymore. I miss her."

"Oh. I don't have any brothers or sisters, it's just me," I replied.

At the end of the day we travelled back on the bus together and she got off long before me. None of the other kids spoke to me although they whispered a lot behind their hands, their eyes looking my way, but I just ignored them.

When the bus stopped at the top of the lane to Edith's house there was no one to greet me. Some of the other kids had mums or dads at their stop who bundled them up into a hug. I just made my way down the lane to the house. Edith was always there, she left the house only once a day, every day, to go to church and then once a week to the grocery store. Why someone would want to go to church every day was beyond me, I'd never been to a church before.

Edith had a list of things I had to do, she had written them down on a large piece of paper that she pinned up on the kitchen wall. It would change from day to day but some of the things remained the same. I had to sweep the front yard, start repainting the wooden rails around the porch and make sure there were enough logs cut and stacked for winter. Sawing logs was a new one to me, I would find the fallen branches in the woods and drag them until sweat dripped off my brow, all the way back to the house.

Then I would saw them into smaller pieces until blisters formed on my hands. They then had to be chopped in half and luckily, she had a splitter. The logs had to be exactly the same size, ready for storing for the fire or the stove, or she would make me do them again. It never dawned on me that someone of my age should not be doing these things. I would have to help sweep the house as there were no carpets anywhere, the occasional rug but otherwise it was just wooden floors throughout. I would then clean the kitchen, wash the dishes each night and finally, exhausted, I did my homework and fell into bed. I didn't mind being busy, it kept me warm. Even in the summer the house was always chilly and Edith wouldn't have the fire going. The warmest place was either fully clothed under my quilt or in front of the stove.

Edith and I never really spoke much, she never asked me about my day, what I had done at school. She would sit at her desk each night and read from her bible, aloud. I would sit and listen, there was not much else I could do really. She didn't have a TV to watch and other than my school book, I had nothing to read. Sometimes she would read then ask me questions, if I couldn't answer she would get cross. She would squint her eyes at me, tut and read the passage again, slower.

****

The first time she beat me was about a month after I had arrived. It was when I was late home from school. The bus had a flat so we didn't leave at our usual time. By the time I had arrived home, I was fifteen minutes late. Edith was at the end of the lane, at the stop waiting for me. I smiled when we arrived, it was unusual but good to see her. My smile soon faded when I saw the look in her eyes, she meant me harm, I could tell.

She dragged me by the arm from the bus in front of everyone, her fingers dug into my skin and my face burnt with embarrassment. She pushed me in front of her, forcing me to march the path to the house and then I heard it, a whoosh, followed by a sting across my back. The buckle end of a belt bit into my skin. I turned in shock, no one had ever hit me before and she lashed out again, catching my side, then my stomach.

"I know what you are, what you are up to," she screamed at me, repeatedly.

As quick as I stumbled backwards, she came forwards, swinging her arm, the belt wrapped around her hand and the end catching any part of my body it could. She was cursing me but I didn't understand what she was saying. This could not be because I was late, it was not my fault after all.

I held my hands over the areas she had already hit, trying to take away the pain and ran to the house. When I got on with my chores she stopped but she took up her bible and starting reading aloud to me, following me from room to room. I didn't cry, in hindsight, I didn't have the ability to. I guessed I must have cried as a baby but my mum hated it if I cried and soon enough I learnt not to.

I went to bed that day without any dinner, hungry and confused. What had I done that had deserved that beating? As I lay on my bed the only comfort I got were my thoughts of a previous life, back in England. Whether my mum and dad were good or bad, whether they left me alone or not, it was better than where I was.

The following morning as I dressed I noticed a clear liquid weeping from the cut on my side. I tried to wipe it with tissue but it stung. I pulled on my school shirt and watched it darken as the liquid soaked into it. My back hurt, my body was stiff and it was an effort to walk up the lane to catch the bus. Every step I took made the shirt rub against my wounds.

I took my seat, quietly, next to Cara.

"Are you okay?" she asked.

I just nodded. I was too embarrassed to say anything. We got through the morning, although I fidgeted on my chair and the

Father was constantly yelling at me to sit still. At lunch time, Cara pulled at the back of my shirt. I winced, the shirt had stuck to my cuts and as it pulled away, one had started to bleed. She held the back of my shirt and just looked at me for a while.

"Come with me," she said.

We snuck back into the school, into the toilet where she wet some tissue and wiped my side. The cold water was soothing. We didn't speak but I knew she understood what had happened.

"It stops hurting after a while," she said softly and we left for class.

I can't say the beatings were a daily thing but it seemed that at least every other day there would be a problem and I would take the punishment for it. Sometimes she would come back from church and beat me for no reason. She started to make me sit at her feet and she would preach the bible at me, with one hand on my forehead. What she was doing, I had no idea.

"Submit yourself therefore to God. Resist the devil, and he will flee from you," she would say.

She would close her eyes and rock back and forth, her hand never leaving my forehead as she seemed to be chanting. Sometimes I couldn't hear, she would mumble and other times she would shout out loud. The same thing, repeatedly. I didn't know what her words meant. She talked about the devil a lot.

My life consisted of going to school and coming back to the house, I would never refer to it as home, being beaten and if not beaten then being preached to. At one point Edith had grabbed me by the shoulders, forced me to my knees in front of her and announced that I was the devil. She wanted to help me, to get the devil out of me, make me pure. She told me that my parents were dead because of me, because I had the devil inside. When she said those things my hands would shake with fear. I wasn't sure what I was scared of though, being the devil or her.

****

Cara and I became best friends. She would help me up from my chair when the bruises and the welts from the belt stung on the back of my legs and made me stiff. She would pick leaves from a prickly plant, slice them open and make me rub the sticky, smelly stuff inside, on my cuts. I would do the same for her. Every day that I went to school in pain, so did she. We only ever had one conversation about it.

“Who does this to you?” I had asked her one day.

She had a bruise on her cheek, the skin grazed and when she sat and her skirt raised, I could see bruising on her thighs. I wasn’t trying to look at her legs but the marks looked just like handprints. She had tried to pull her skirt down when she noticed me looking.

“My dad,” she whispered. “He does things to me but you mustn’t tell anyone, promise me.”

“What does he do?” I asked.

“He touches me, down there, and hits me if I cry.” She pointed between her thighs.

“He’s not allowed to do that though,” I said.

She just shrugged her shoulders.

“Don’t you tell your mum?” I asked.

“I did once, he told her I was a dirty little liar and then he killed my cat. He drowned her in the water butt, she had babies and I tried to help them but they needed their momma’s milk.”

Her eyes filled with tears at the memory. We linked our little fingers and made a promise to each other that we wouldn’t tell because, I guessed, we knew if we did, things would get worse.

It was at that time that I started to feel hatred. For Cara’s dad, for my aunt, for my parents, for my teacher, for everyone. The only time this boiling inside me ceased was when I was with Cara, she made me feel calm. Even at the age I was then I knew what was happening to her and I felt angry that I was too young and powerless to stop it.

****

I had been with Edith for just under a couple of years and I hated her, and where I was, with every fibre of my being. Every time I looked at her I would get a taste in my mouth, like after I had been sick, and I would have to swallow hard to get rid of it. I knew then that was what hatred tasted like.

"Are you the devil?" I would ask myself as I looked in the dirty, cracked mirror in the bathroom.

The face that stared back at me, the black eyes, for a while was unsure. If Edith was so sure she must be right. She was a church goer, so she must know what she was talking about. For a while I willingly sat at her feet, I didn't want to be the devil. I would let her beat me, berate and cleanse me until I was pure again. However, there were times when I hoped she was right. If I was the devil I might have special powers to make it stop. I might have special powers to stop what was happening to Cara. Somewhere inside me I had this feeling of really wanting to hurt Edith, the way she hurt me, but I never did. I would dream of putting my hands around her scrawny neck and squeezing until she couldn't breathe. I could picture her face, the fear in her bulging eyes. I could feel her hands on mine trying to pull them away, her dirty nails scraping my skin and I could smell death as she took her last breath.

I wanted her to feel how I did inside, the sadness, the pain and the confusion. I wanted her to feel the ache in my stomach that would never go away and I wanted her to feel the loneliness I felt. I began to hate school as well which did upset me. People kept their distance, but they whispered about me.

"Why don't they talk to me?" I asked one time, looking around the lunch hall.

"Because they're scared of you," Cara said, quite matter of fact.

"You talk to me though."

"Because, silly, you don't scare me," she replied.

"I don't mean to scare people, what are they scared of?"

"Your eyes. You have the black eyes, that's what scares them. You like, stare at people."

Well, I couldn't help the colour of my eyes, could I. I can't help if I stare at people, I am only trying to see if I can work out if they mean me harm, that's all.

****

As fall turned into winter, the beatings got worse. It seemed to be my fault the plumbing froze or the stove didn't work, I had cursed this house she would scream at me. It was my fault the newly painted porch made the rest of the house look shabby. It was my fault the logs were too big and they didn't stack well enough. However, as she, and I, got older, I got wiser. I managed to hide from her for a while, I had my camp in the woods, somewhere she couldn't find me.

I would come home from school, quickly do my chores and head out to the woods. I liked being outdoors, if I could I would live there forever. It was peaceful, it was clean and it was exactly as it should be. I had spent the whole summer making my camp. I nailed wood to the trees to make a frame and covered it with an old tarpaulin I had found. It was quiet and peaceful. If Cara managed to get out after school, she would meet me there. We would sit and plan our escape. We would talk about imaginary places where we would live together. I told her how we would stow away on a plane and I would take her back to Sarah's. I told her all about Benny and that we could take him for walks in the park, we could throw his ball and wait for him to bring it back. She would love being at Sarah's. I would even let her bring that box of dolls out from under the bed.

"Do you speak to Sarah?" Cara had asked me one time.

"No, I don't know if she knows where I am. I would like to though, I miss her."

I would have loved to have asked my aunt if I could call Sarah but, somehow, I knew she wouldn't allow it. She had a telephone in the house but it was never used. There was never any mention of my life in England, it was as if it hadn't existed.

Time after time Cara and I talked about running away. I knew we could do it but she was too scared to try. I would spend hours trying to convince her that I would take care of her. I would never beat her, I would hunt to make sure we had food and we could live in the woods forever. I made bows and arrows, I sharpened stones until they could prick my skin, like a knife. I made a pillow for her out of leaves and dried grass that, when she was really sad, she would lay her head on and close her eyes. As she rested her body, I carved our initials into a tree trunk, a symbol that we would be friends forever. I would watch her, that anger boiling away under the surface at what had happened to her. I was only nine years old.

I would sleep outdoors some nights, wrapped up in a blanket I had stolen from the house and watch the night sky, the stars, cursing my parents for being dead and leaving me in his hell hole. Sometimes my chest would hurt with the intensity of it all. I wanted to feel something else, anything, and even when I punched the tree trunk over and over and watched my knuckles bleed, I felt no pain, nothing but this emptiness inside. It was like I was hollow and if I beat my chest it echoed.

What I liked most about being outdoors was that it was constant. The leaves fell at the same time of the year, the flowers opened when they should. I had a sense of time, of purpose when I stayed outside. Inside the house it was too unpredictable, outside I knew exactly what was going to happen and when.

Some days I would pack my school back pack with food I had stolen. I knew Cara and I could hide away in the woods for however long it took for people to stop looking for us, or so I thought, but we never did. Cara would get upset and cry when I tried to persuade her to run away. I hated to make her cry. Later in life I would often wonder why I stayed for as long as I had, why I endured what I did. But in my heart I knew, I only stayed because of Cara, she needed me and I needed her.

I turned ten with no notice from anyone that it was my birthday. It was pure luck that I had found out. I'd found some papers when I was tidying the lounge, they mentioned the house my mother had owned, the fact that it had been sold a long time ago. I wondered what had happened to the money. However, there was my name and my date of birth. No one had celebrated my birthday for years, so it was good to read that day was special. I was good at math, I added up the years I was born and realised I was ten years old. Wow, double figures already.

That morning I boarded the bus and took my usual seat next to Cara. She didn't greet me with the smile she usually did. Instead her head was turned to the window.

"It's my birthday today, I'm ten," I told her.

When she did turn to me, her eye was black and closed, her lip split. Tears rolled down her cheeks, yet she smiled.

"Happy birthday, Robert," she said.

I just sat and stared. She shook her head gently, a silent ask for me not to talk about it before she turned her face back to the window. I picked up her hand and held it in mine, I didn't care who saw, who sniggered. She was my best friend and I didn't know how to help her.

Cara was quiet for most of the day but at lunchtime we sat together and she shared her lunch with me. After we had eaten she took my hand and we wandered to the prickly plants by the small copse at the back of the school. I knew those plants to be Aloe Vera and, not that it ever worked, the sticky stuff inside was meant to heal our cuts. Cara turned to me and raised her skirt. Not only were her legs covered in bruises but her white panties were stained red. I stared, open mouthed, not sure if I was to say anything or not. The blood had smeared down her thighs. I watched her body start to shake, she wrapped her arms around herself and for the first time she cried, really cried. I wanted to hold her, to comfort her, but as I moved towards her she backed away.

"My tummy hurts," she whispered.

"Did he do that?" I asked, my voice cracking on every word.

She didn't answer, she didn't need to. Her lip had started to bleed a little, a small trickle of blood ran down to her chin. As she wiped at it, she smeared it across her face. The tears that were rolling down her cheeks left a clean line through the blood. I was horrified, the sight of her blood stained body stayed with me for many years after.

"I'm going to kill him," I shouted, and I turned and ran.

I heard her calling me, begging me to come back and as I ran Father Peters stepped from the church into my path.

"Where do you think you are going?" he asked.

"Look at her," I screamed. "Look at what he did to her."

"It's not your business, Robert," he said.

"She's my friend and she's hurt."

He reached out and grabbed my arms. I fought, shouting and screaming at him. I was way stronger than he was and I managed to push him away. He stumbled and fell, landing on the dirt path. As I turned to continue my journey I caught sight of

Cara, she was bent over holding her stomach and calling my name. It pulled me up short and I walked back to her. My chest hurt with the anger, my breathing was rapid and I clenched my fists as tight as I could.

“Please, Robert, don’t go. He’ll kill me if you do. You promised me you wouldn’t tell, you promised,” she said between her sobs.

“I’m not going anywhere, Cara. Not without you, anyway,” I said. “Please, let’s run, now. I’ll look after you, I won’t let anyone hurt you, ever again,” I begged.

She just shook her head, resigned to her fate, I guessed. We knelt together on the dusty, dried grass and I held her. By now a crowd had formed, the other kids stood around us. No one spoke and when I looked at them, the hatred must have blazed from my eyes as they backed away. Some time later I heard a man’s voice, calling Cara. Before she stood, she placed her hand on my cheek wiping away a tear and then she got up and walked away. I stayed kneeling where I was, crying for the first time ever and finally broken.

****

I never saw Cara again. She didn’t get on the bus the following morning, or the one after and I missed her. I walked to where she lived night after night, to see if I could find her. There was no sign of her anywhere. She had been the only friend I’d ever had. The only person that had been kind to me, that played with me, that talked to me even. I knew she hadn’t moved away, I still saw her parents sometimes, but never Cara. I asked my aunt once, I wanted to know what had happened to her. I don’t know why I asked, because I knew, deep down I knew what had happened. I received the worst beating ever that day and was told not to ask questions. I couldn’t walk without being hunched over, the scratchy material of my school shirt constantly rubbed at the welts which bled and wept for days. At night I would look up at the stars and wonder if she was looking down at me.

In one way I was envious of Cara, she had escaped her misery, her pain. She was free from it all and I wished I was with her. In my ten year old mind it was better to be dead than alive and beaten.

Chapter Two

For a few weeks after Cara's disappearance, the kids, the teachers, Father Peters, all kept their distance from me. If I walked towards a crowd it parted and silence fell. Eyes followed me wherever I went. Kids whispered about me but everyone left me alone. Finally I began to understand their fear of me and I used that to my advantage. I remember someone wanted to take my lunch, it was the only meal I was likely to get that day. My aunt had stopped cooking and I was never allowed to help myself. The kid came and stood beside me while I sat at the table in the lunch hall, taunting and calling me names.

"Hey, dumb ass, weirdo," he said, the other kids laughed, nervously.

"Are you listening to me, Child of Satan?" he taunted, turning towards his friends with a cocky grin.

Child of Satan, oh come on, you can do better than that, I'd thought. So I stood, I was taller, broader, way stronger and the strange thing was, all I had to do was to look into his eyes. I saw all I needed to know. He was a coward, a bully, a beaten kid just like me. I saw him shake, I saw him wet his pants and I hadn't said a word. No one ever bothered me again after that.

I barely spoke, other than to answer a question the teacher had asked with a one word answer. I had nothing to say to anyone. I was scared. If I opened my mouth, I was scared what would come out. The vile words that swam constantly around my head would spew out like lava from a volcano and I wouldn't be able to stop it. If I voiced how I felt, well, all hell would be let loose.

****

One afternoon I arrived home on the bus. As I climbed the steps of the porch I heard voices. We had a visitor and we never had visitors. It was Father Peters, he had come to speak with Edith. They sat and chatted in the lounge for a long time before calling me into the room.

"Robert, Father Peters wants to have a chat with you," Edith had said.

I sat, quietly looking at him. He might be a priest but I had the measure of him. He was not a good man, not a man of God, by any means.

"Robert, people are concerned about you. You seemed to have scared a few of your classmates," he said.

No shit, Sherlock, I thought, remembering a phrase I had heard on TV once, many years ago.

"Do you want to talk about it?" he asked, and I noticed a shake to his hands.

"I don't know why people are scared of me, Cara wasn't," I said, deliberately mentioning her name.

"I don't think we should be speaking about Cara and I also think it might be good if you come to church more often," he replied.

I was already dragged there at the weekends, sitting on a hard cold bench, listening to tons of drivel for what seemed like hours.

"Why would I do that?" I asked. I didn't know where the question had come from really.

"Well, you might find it a comfort," he said.

I leant forward on the sofa, looking at him, unblinking. "A comfort? From what Father?" I asked, my voice surprisingly steady and low despite the rage I felt inside.

Did he know? Did he know how regularly I was beaten with that fucking belt, preached to from that fucking bible by that fucking mad, old woman? Did he know Cara had been raped then later, beaten to death by her father? Did he know most of the kids in the school came every day with fresh bruises to their faces, to their arms? Of course he fucking knew. And he knew that I knew, too.

A smirk formed across my lips, I had a moment of clarity.

"What is it, Robert? What do you want to say?" he asked, his cup rattling on his saucer.

"You will fucking burn in hell and so will she," I said slowly, my eyes moving to where Edith sat.

"You think you know me? You don't know shit, but one day you will."

Where had that come from? I looked at the wide eyes of both the Father and my aunt. I loved the words shit and fuck. I had heard them at school recently and vowed to use them at every opportunity.

"What are...? Err, why do you say that?" he asked, his voice shaking, stammering.

"You know what goes on here and you do nothing to stop it. You know what happened to Cara and you did nothing to stop it. Someday you'll pay for those sins, I can promise you that," I said.

I got up and walked out of the room, into the woods, the only place I felt safe, secure and the place I knew no one would visit. Edith would never have come looking for me, I could be there all night and sometimes I had, and she'd not noticed nor cared.

What I had said was wrong, wrong in that it meant the beatings became more frequent. I was told it was for my own good, to make me better. I often wondered why I didn't stop her, I was bigger, stronger, I could have easily snatched that belt from her hands. Yet I sat night after night on the cold, hard, lounge floor with her sitting on the sofa reading the bible to me. I knew the fucking thing back to front and I did not believe one word of it. I was just biding my time.

I became immune to the beatings, I would switch my brain off. I heard nothing. I felt nothing. I would look at my aunt, I would see her mouth moving but I didn't hear the words anymore. I just stared at her and sometimes I smiled. The more I smiled, the more fear showed in her eyes and the more slaps from the belt I got. I didn't care anymore. I just stood still, no attempt to run or try to get away and let her get on with it. As Cara had told me it would, that belt had stopped hurting my skin a long time ago.

I found it amusing that Edith talked about and to God. There was no God. If there was, what a cruel, sadistic, evil thing he was. Would a God kill my mum and dad, Cara, have me left here to be beaten until my skin scarred, my body was left covered in bruises? Would He leave me not able to sleep because of one weeping, infected cut or another? Would a God have me slave for a woman who thought she was divine and who thought I was the devil? No, no God would do that and on my eleventh birthday, I finally cracked.

****

I don't know whether I really meant for it to happen. All I wanted was to stop her beating me, to stop her reading the pile of shit she preached at me. One night I took her bibles, every one I could find, the belt she used and put them in a pile on the floor, in the basement. I found a can of gasoline which I splashed over them and I stood back. I lit a match, watched the flame grow stronger and then I dropped it onto that pile I associated with pain and hatred and suffering.

I watched it ignite, fascinated by the flames, by the colour of the burning books and the smell of scorched leather. I stood back and watched as the fire spread along the line of gasoline I had dripped until it caught the can and the pile of old newspapers. I watched the whole basement catch light. I left the house, quite calmly and made my way outside. I was transfixed by the crackling sounds, the smell of burning wood and the sight as the fire took hold, licking its way over the house and lighting up the night sky. It was a beautiful sight. I watched the house burn, knowing she was in there and I did nothing to save her. I felt nothing. The last tiniest bit of emotion I was able to feel, shut down that day. The aching in my stomach, the pain in my heart, the loneliness I felt, it all disappeared. I was happily numb. I simply made my way into the woods and to the safety of my camp.

I slept, probably the best night's sleep I'd had in ages. No worrying that she would come for me in the night to make me kneel at my bed and pray with her. No worrying about the sound of the belt as it whooshed through the air before connecting with my body. No worrying about the words that came out of her mouth, how terrible I was, how evil I was, how my parents had died because of me.

In the morning I crept to the edge of the woods. People were milling around, kicking through the still hot embers of what used to be a house. The fire truck had been there during the night but it had been too late. The house was just a pile of ash and scorched wood. I saw the police, I saw the Father and I stayed exactly where I was. I didn't come forward and tell anyone what had happened, I waited for hours until the coast was clear and then I turned and walked away.

I walked, I hitched a lift where I could, and I jumped into the back of a pick up without the driver knowing until I eventually ended up in a city. I had no idea where I was, but all I knew was that it was better than where I had just come from.

****

It was night by the time I had arrived, I'd travelled all day. I was hungry and I was cold. I found a river, a large one and followed it until I came to a bridge where I settled underneath. I pulled my jumper around me as tight as I could, trying to gain some warmth from that threadbare covering. I hugged my legs close to me, my head resting on my knees and I closed my eyes, I was so tired.

I heard noises, a young voice and waking, I saw a boy struggling to hold onto a plastic bag, two older kids trying to snatch it away. I saw the young boy fight with all his might and a tear run down his grubby face. I stood and walked to the end of the bridge, to where the commotion was. The two older boys stopped and watched me approach.

"Fuck off friend, if you know what's good for you," one said.

I carried on towards them. What they were doing was wrong and I wanted to stop it. I felt no fear and it wasn't until I was close that they seemed to falter, their bravado wavering.

"I'm not your friend. Now, leave him alone," I said, and I was surprised by my voice.

I hadn't really spoken to anyone for ages and I was taken aback by how deep it sounded, made worse by the echo bouncing off the walls. I carried on walking, closer and closer to them. I looked them straight in the eye and I saw that they too were cowards, they couldn't hurt me. I was taller, stronger and I knew that if they wanted to hit me, they could never do worse than what I had already suffered.

No blow to my body would ever hurt me the way that belt did, the way my aunt had, the way my parents had. There was nothing those boys, or anyone for that matter, could do to me and they knew it. I watched them raise their hands and back off before turning to run when they were a safe distance away. In one way I was totally fearless but I was also emotionless, I simply didn't care and it must have showed on my face.

"Thanks," the kid said.

I didn't reply, just gave him a small smile. When I looked closely at him, I realised he was my age, just a lot smaller. No doubt he hadn't had to cut logs every day of his life. I turned to walk back to where I had come from and he followed. I hadn't wanted him to follow, I only wanted to stop him getting beaten, to be able to hold onto whatever was in his bag. I sat and he slid down the wall beside me.

"I'm Travis," he said, I just nodded.

We sat in silence for a while until eventually he asked, "Are you hungry, I have some food?"

I was starving. I gratefully accepted the bread roll from his bag and we ate, again in silence, together.

"What are you doing here?" he asked, eventually.

"Same as you, I guess," I replied.

"You can't stay here tonight, the cops will show anytime. This is the place the drunks come and they get moved on. Half the time the cops end up fishing them out of the river, they get so drunk they fall in," he told me. "But if you want, you can come to where I sleep."

He got up and waited for me. He had dark blond hair and blue eyes. His jeans were torn and his T-shirt grubby. He had a leather jacket that he pulled around himself for warmth, his sneakers though, looked new. Seeing me staring at them, he told me he had stolen them from a local store, had to do with two different sizes though. We made our way out from under the bridge and followed the river bank for a while.

"What's this city?" I asked, looking around.

We were walking along the sidewalk, cars passing us in different directions, their headlights blazing like angry eyes. People rushed about, dodging us, tutting if we hadn't moved out of their way fast enough.

"Are you kidding me?" he replied.

"Do I look like I am kidding you?" I was tired, cold and really not in the mood.

"Well, no you don't. Welcome to the home of the President of the United States, Washington, DC," he said proudly and waving his arms around.

Washington, wow. I hadn't taken too much notice of roads signs, hiding out in the back of the truck on the way there. I'd never been to DC before, I'd never been anywhere for that matter, but I wouldn't mind seeing the White House, I'd thought.

"You have a strange accent, where are you from?" he asked.

"I came from England four years ago, lived in Pittsburgh until yesterday."

I didn't feel there was any need to lie to him, what would he do with that information? I guess my accent must have changed over the years, I couldn't tell myself. Perhaps it was a mix of English and American.

"What about you?"

"My mom and dad came from Northern Ireland but I was born here, well, in New York," he said.

We had been walking for a while until we eventually came to an alleyway between two take out shops. Ducking down this alley, I noticed other people either curled up on cardboard near dumpsters or wrapped in dirty coats and blankets in doorways. At the bottom of this alleyway, before it opened up into another street, I saw a small gang of kids. Well, I say kids, they looked more my size which meant they were older than me and Travis. He greeted them.

"Well, what did you get?" they asked, as they rummaged through the bag he held.

Taking whatever food they wanted, they turned their backs on him, huddling together to eat. Travis gestured that we should sit on a stone step, the back entrance to somewhere, a little way from the group.

“What’s with your friend?” one of them said, noticing I was watching them and they sauntered over.

“He’s cool, leave him alone,” Travis said.

“Why are you staring at me?” he asked. I guessed him to be about sixteen, a cigarette hung from his lip.

I didn’t answer, there really was no need. He kicked his foot out, catching mine.

“I’m talking to you,” he said. Finally I stood up, towering over him and took a step forwards.

“If I want to look at you, I will,” I said, staring him down, there was no way I would back off.

I watched him shrivel away from me, his cigarette drop to the floor. That was the second time that had happened that day and I felt a sense of something that I couldn’t put my finger on, I liked it though. I had so much anger inside me, it felt like it was flowing out of my pores. I’d never been one to shout or fight back and for some reason, it was looking like I would never have to.

“Wow, man, that’s cool. You scared him off and he’s a right fucker,” Travis said, smiling.

I returned to the step, this would have to do for the night. However, I would need to find somewhere a little nicer, somewhere that didn’t smell of piss. I could already sleep with my ears active, I’d learnt to do that in case Edith came into my room, back in Sterling. I settled my back against the door jam and closed my eyes.

“I’m Robert,” I said to Travis as he settled down next to me.

I woke to shouts, something foreign. Someone had opened the door I was leaning against and with a broom, was ushering us out of the way. We jumped up and ran, out of the alley into the morning daylight. It was the first time I had been to any city and I was amazed at the amount of cars, of people walking with a purpose.

Some were in suits making their way to work and as we weaved our way in and out of the throng of people, some would look at us with disdain, with disgust in their eyes. It was those people that I hated the most. Those people that I would stop and stare back at until they felt uncomfortable enough to look away and scurry on, like little rats. My stomach was rumbling, I needed something to eat, but I had no money.

"Breakfast?" Travis asked, a smile on his face, his eyes twinkling with mischief.

"Sure, but I don't have any money," I replied.

"This is the land of opportunity," he said. "We don't need money."

I followed him to a street vendor selling donuts. The vendor obviously saw us coming, Travis stood out like a sore thumb. As brazen as you like, Travis asked him if he had any donuts he was going to throw away and, if so, could we have them, we were hungry. To my surprise and to the surprise of the vendor, who was expecting Travis to try and steal something, he handed over two donuts. We stuffed them in our mouths quickly.

"Thank you, mister," he said. "That was really kind of you."

Before he had finished his sentence he stole a bag of them from the counter top and we ran, laughing, through the streets.

"Easy," he said, sharing the donuts with me. "If I ask for stuff sometimes they give it to me and when they do, they don't expect me to pinch it after," he added, laughing.

He was quite a strange person and I began to like him. He told me that he had run away from home a while ago, he had been on the streets for about a year. His parents were still around, his dad and brothers were drunks who beat him and his mum until one day he walked out. He had convinced his sister's dumb boyfriend to let him ride with him to Washington and didn't go back.

"What's your story?" he asked.

"Similar. My parents died, I came here to live with an aunt. She thought she could beat the devil out of me and one day I had enough. I burnt down her house and here I am," I replied. I had purposely omitted the part about killing her.

He didn't look shocked, he simply nodded as if he understood. He was easy to get on with, he showed me around the city, well, as much as his little legs would allow. We stood outside the White House and looked through the iron railings. The head of the USA lived there and I wondered, if he was looking out, did he see two dirty, homeless kids right on his doorstep and was he ashamed of that?

"If I was the President, no kid would live on the street," I said. I spat on his lawn and walked away.

Since, at that moment, I looked a little cleaner than Travis, the next dinner run was mine. To be honest, it wasn't hard. Pick a small grocery store where the owner was behind the large counter, designed to stop me getting to the other side but equally, it stopped them getting to me. I would wander around picking up things and placing them in my basket as if I was supposed to be there. Once I neared the check out I would make a run for it. I became an expert at shoplifting although sometimes someone would intervene and grab the basket but never me. Often, I simply walked out without anyone really noticing. On the odd occasion that I was caught, generally one look had them backing off.

I started to understand what this thing was, what made people back away from me. The lack of fear, the emotionless look on my face scared them and I was glad of that. Being able to scare people without doing anything gave me a sense of power, a crucial survival tactic. Travis and I became very good friends. He was fun, he was cheeky but he wouldn't survive long term. He had exhausted the people he could rob for food so I made some plans for us.

First, we needed some clean clothes. We couldn't enter any store without raising suspicion because of how we looked and probably how we smelt. Arriving at a local hardware store that sold pretty much everything, we entered separately. With two of us it was easy. I walked purposefully to the counter and asked for some advice.

"Sir, my dad asked me to come and talk to you. We have a splitter at home and it's not working properly. He wants to know whether we should repair or replace it," I said.

"What kind do you have?" he asked, probably testing me.

"It's a Woodstar but quite old. The blade has been sharpened but it's just not splitting right through."

We had a conversation about the blade, maybe the angle was off and he asked if the splitter had been dropped. Because I knew the piece of machinery it was easy to keep him distracted.

"Okay, let's have a look and see if we can find a replacement for your dad," he said.

I had as long a conversation with the store keeper as I could. In the meantime, Travis exchanged his T-shirt for one of the same colour, placing a slightly larger one over the top, he hid two pairs of pants under his jacket and whilst I was shown some brochures on new blades, he made his way out the door. I thanked the guy, took the brochures and promised to return later that day. I found us a local swimming baths, we snuck in and I made him take a shower. We had no towels so we sat and drip dried but at least our hair and our bodies were clean.

"Well, that was easy," Travis said as we sat on a bench. "I wonder if we could open those lockers."

"Trav, in the corner of the room, see, there's a camera. We won't get out of this door before we got caught," I replied.

"Oh, so someone is looking at us, sitting here butt naked right now. Perverts," he said with a laugh.

Travis was always laughing and being with him made me feel better. He was starting to have the same effect on me as Cara had, he calmed the anger inside me. The vile words that still swum around my head started to lessen and I could think clearer.

"I don't suppose someone is looking at us," I said, shaking my head. "Just get dressed and let's get out of here."

The difference when we wore clean clothes was unbelievable. No longer did we receive the looks of disgust, but perhaps a smile as we bade good morning to someone. I vowed from that day that people would never look at me in disgust again.

"Why does it bother you, what these people think of us?" Travis had asked.

"Because, Trav, we might not be as fortunate as them but there's no reason to be disrespectful, no reason to be disgusted by us," I informed him.

****

We had been together for a couple of months, hanging about, trying not to get picked up by the cops or perverts when an opportunity arose. Not one I would normally like to have taken but I was hungry, Travis was hungry but also he was sick. He needed some medicine. Not that I was a doctor but he sounded like he could do with something for his chest, he had a terrible cough and he had a fever. His forehead was covered in beads of sweat and he winced, holding his sides every time he coughed.

A woman walked past me distracted, searching in her handbag for something and allowing one arm of the bag to fall down her shoulder. Easy pickings. I snatched the purse that was sitting, conveniently, at the top. She gave chase for a little while, calling out to me. I looked over my shoulder and I saw her crouch down on that cold, dirty sidewalk. People strolled past her as if she was nothing. No one stopped to help and I saw a tear fall from her eye. I felt like a complete dick. I walked back and handed her the purse. She looked at me, she had dark brown eyes, not as dark as mine of course but I saw a sadness and a kindness in them. She was tired, she had a tired soul. I bent down, held out my hand to her and helped her to her feet. She smoothed down her dress and placed her purse back in her bag.

"My friend is sick, I needed money for medicine," I said, to explain my actions.

"Where is your friend?" she asked.

"Not far," I replied, not wanting to give away our location.

"Can I see him? I might be able to help."

"Yeah lady, then you'll be back with the cops," I said, standing tall.

I could see a flicker of fear in her eyes. I loved to see that normally but not in her case, I didn't want her to fear me. There was something about her, something I didn't understand but I knew I could trust her.

"Come on," I said, and she followed me.

Travis was wrapped up in a blanket I had stolen, he was not asleep but had his eyes shut. No one ever *slept* on the streets, you couldn't afford to. It was too dangerous once the sun set, once the street lights lit and once the normal people had left it. So, no, we never slept as such, just dozed enough for our bodies to repair of whatever exhaustion we had met with that day. She bent down to him and placed her hand on his burning forehead.

“He’s so hot, he must have a fever,” she said.

She took out her purse and handed me a $10 bill.

“You’re right, he needs medicine. Just around the block is a pharmacy. Ask them for paracetamol and get a bottle of water too,” she said.

I rushed away knowing that she would still be there when I got back. I bought what she asked for and it felt odd. It was the first time I had ever entered a store with money and paid for something.

I ran back as fast as I could and she was still there. She told me that he needed the paracetamol to bring the fever down and to make sure he had regular sips of water. She also said that she would be back later with some food. It wasn’t long before she returned with some hot pies in a bag, some coffee in take out containers and it was the best meal we’d ever had.

“Will you be here tomorrow?” she asked.

“Yeah, unless the cops come, then we might have to move,” I replied.

Until Travis was well, I was hoping we weren’t going anywhere. If the cops came, he wasn’t well enough to run and there was no way we wanted to get caught. Some of the other kids on the street had told us the horror stories of what happened in the cells or the homes they had been placed in.

As she left I asked her, “What’s your name, lady?”

“Evelyn,” she replied. “But you can call me Ev if you want. And what do I call you?” she asked.

“Robert Stone, at your service,” I said, bowing at the waist. “And this here, is Travis.”

From that day forwards Travis and I saw Evelyn nearly every day.

Travis got well, Ev came by frequently to check on us, making sure we had something to eat. She worked in a local office, typing and stuff she’d told me. She would pick up something for us on her way to work and sometimes we would walk with her. Often, we would wait for her at the end of the day, hanging around outside her office, smiling when we saw her then walking her home. We would chat about our day and she would be doubled over with laughter at some of our antics. It didn't take long to see the sadness in her eyes start to fade. I had often wondered what had made her so sad, but never asked.

****

It was a few months later, on a sunny day, mid August, when our lives changed. I went into a small grocery store without thinking about how many times we had hit it, all I wanted was some water, something to drink. I walked into the store, snatched a couple of bottles from a shelf and ran for the door. I noticed a shadow fall across the floor in front of the doorway and as I came to an abrupt halt, I looked up into the brown eyes of a huge guy. Behind him were two others. He had a smile on his face, but with one large hand he grabbed me by the scruff of my neck and turning me around, he made me place the bottles of water back on the shelf.

I didn't fight as such, that was pointless, he was larger and stronger than I was, but I would not back down. As much as he stared at me, I would not look away. I was not ashamed of what I had done, I was surviving that's all. His grip released on my collar and I straightened my shirt. I held out my hand to him, which he took.

"Robert Stone," I introduced myself. He had no need to return his name, I knew exactly who he was.

He laughed. Here was some kid, shaking his hand like a man, staring him down without a shred of fear in my eyes, I guessed that amused him. He admired me, he told me many years later, for that.

"So you're Robert Stone. I've been looking for you," he said. "You best follow me kid, and where's your partner in crime?"

Guiseppi took me back to his office with him. It was only a short walk to a doorway in between two stores and up a flight of stairs. Travis followed behind. We had developed a code as such, a slight nod of the head or a gesture of our hands. I'd told him to hold back until I knew what we were dealing with. What I noticed was, as we walked, people either moved out of Guiseppi's way or practically fell over themselves wanting to shake his hand.

Guiseppi opened the door into a room with barely any light, bars at the cracked, dirty windows and people sitting about smoking or drinking. It looked like a sleaze bar and the place stank of stale cigarettes and booze. I wrinkled my nose.

"Nice place you got here," I said, sarcastically.

"Says he, whose office is a doorstep in an alley."

"At least I keep it clean, I know where everything is," I said, a slight smile playing across my lips.

"If you pay us, me and my friend will clean this place up," I added, looking around.

"And what kind of payment do you want?" he asked, amused by me.

"$5 each, which you will see once we're done, will be a bargain."

So started our careers with Guiseppi Morietti, an Italian immigrant from Naples, the local kingpin, the gangland boss and, as I found out later, Evelyn's father.

Travis and I spent the next day cleaning the office. We lugged out some old, broken furniture which we left on the sidewalk, then swept and cleaned the whole place. Cleaning was something I had done every day when I lived in Sterling. Cleaning was something Travis had never done and he grumbled the whole day. For that we received our $5 each, a huge amount of money, or so we thought. I learnt one valuable lesson that day, I had sold us too cheap.

"Well, well, you did good, kid," Guiseppi said when he returned, flanked by two of the largest guys I had ever seen.

"Of course we did. Now, if you have any other jobs we can do?" I replied.

He thought for a moment. "Come back tomorrow, early," he said, as he dismissed us.

As we turned to leave we saw Evelyn entering the office, she smiled at us.

"Papa, I see you've met Robert and Travis then," she said.

Papa! So her father was the great Guiseppi Morietti. At that moment I was quite glad I had given back her purse. I chuckled and she winked at me as we left.

The first thing Travis did was run to the candy shop. I bought a small writing book and a pen. I had decided that I wanted Joe, as we called him, to hold onto my earnings and I would record every dime, until such a time as I needed it.

The following morning we were there, sitting on the doorstep before anyone arrived. I watched as a huge black car pulled up to the curb. A driver and passenger got out before opening the rear door for Joe to exit and we stood as he made his way towards us.

"If you are going to work for me you need clean clothes," he said, peeling off $50. "Go and get some, then get straight back here."

"Oh man, look at all that money," Travis said as we walked away. "We could live on that for a month."

"No, Trav, we're going to do as he says. We'll buy some clothes and give him back the change."

"Rob, come on, look at it, when are we going to see $50 again," he said.

We bought new jeans, a couple of new T-shirts each, underwear and some sneakers. I asked for a receipt from the store and handed it to Joe with the change once we returned. He took them both with raised eyebrows, surprise registering in his eyes.

"I thought you might not have come back," he said.

"I guess we passed your test then, didn't we," I answered.

We started to run errands, sometimes it was just to collect his dry cleaning or drop off a package to someone and for that we earned. The amount depended on what we did but by the end of a week Travis had nothing and I had $30. I was 12 years old and to me, and back then, that was an extraordinary amount of money. Joe allowed us to sleep at his office. We made up camp beds in a corner and Evelyn had brought us linen and a couple of pillows from their house. She would also, each morning, bring down something for us to eat, returning in the evening with another meal.

Joe had a team of guys around him, some in their twenties, some older. The older guys, Jonathan especially, were fine with us. I guess they humoured us more than anything, the younger ones though, they were a different bunch altogether. Paul was the one I struggled with the most at first, although I was eight years younger, we were about the same size, evenly matched in build but I believed he saw me as a threat somehow. He was shifty, his eyes never met anyone's when he spoke. He always looked as if he had something to hide.

****

The first time I had to hit anyone was when I had to deliver a package and collect a payment for it. Climbing the stairs in a grubby apartment block, I held my breath. The stench of decay and piss overwhelmed me. We arrived at a broken front door, hanging by its brackets and walked in, stepping over garbage bags spewing with rotting food. A skinny guy, older than us was slouched on a couch. He looked to be more stuck to it such was the layer of grime. I handed over the package and was told to, "Now, fuck off."

I stood my ground. "I want the money, you know I can't go back to Guiseppi without your payment," I said, quite calmly.

I didn't know the man's name nor what we had delivered but he laughed at me, not something I liked people doing, it was disrespectful.

"Money," I said, taking a step closer to him and holding out my hand.

Looking in his eyes, all I could see was some faraway look. The guy was obviously on drugs and perhaps that was making him brave. Forget him being scared of me but he should have been scared of Joe, everyone else was.

"Beat it, kid," he said, as he started to open the package. Travis was standing by the doorway, waiting to see how I would respond.

The guy must have been in his twenties and constantly wiping his nose with the back of his hand. He would have looked at me, all of twelve and thought he could have one over on me. But I was much, much stronger. As quick as a flash I pulled back my fist and punched him square in the face. I felt the crunch as his nose broke, a hot liquid run over my fist as the blood squirted and he fell from the couch to his knees, his hands over his face.

Bending down, I grabbed a handful of hair raising his face so he could look at me. "Money, now," I growled.

He gestured with one hand, the other still holding his broken nose. Travis moved to the other side of the room and counted out the notes, taking an extra $10 because of the effort we'd had to exert to complete a simple transaction. We arrived back at Joe's and I handed him the money, bloodied.

"What happened?" he asked, looking at my fist and the money.

"He didn't want to pay so I made him. Travis took an extra $10 for the effort, if you think we deserve it for having to hit the guy, we'll split it, if not, keep it yourself," I said.

Joe looked stunned, as did the guys he always surrounded himself with.

"Let me get this straight. That prick didn't want to pay, so you hit him. You then took an extra $10 which you are asking me to give you, if I think you deserve it."

"Yes," I said, I thought it was quite simple really. "If I hadn't of hit him, you would not have been paid. Not only have we delivered the package, I then had to fight to get the money, that meant an extra job."

He laughed, a real belly laugh. "Kid, with pleasure," he said, as he handed over the money. "Paul, go let that fucker know he always pays," he added.

I had started to keep hold of Travis's money, giving him a daily allowance. If he had it all, it would be spent in minutes and, as I kept telling him, we had to think about the future. Saving money was a good thing, only spend what you need, I'd told him.

"Kid, tomorrow I want you to meet someone," Joe said.

****

We sat in the office the following morning waiting for that big car to arrive. Instead of Joe getting out, we were told to get in. We slid along the smooth leather seats in the rear of the car. I don't think I had ever sat in anything so big. As tall as I was, my feet didn't touch the seats in front. We drove for a short while before we arrived at a slightly run-down building. Entering, I saw that it was a boxing club. A ring dominated the centre of the hall, punch bags and speed balls hung on chains from the ceiling. There were soft mats around and people were working out, some skipping, some lying on their backs having the heavy ball thrown at them and I looked around wide eyed.

"Kids, this is Ted. Ted the kids I told you about," Joe said, by way of an introduction.

Standing in front of me was a man, middle aged I guessed, a broken nose and a cigarette hanging from his lips. His gnarled hand engulfed mine in a shake.

"Ted here used to be one of my best fighters," Joe told us. "He's going to show you some moves, channel that anger of yours a bit better."

Travis and I were shown to a changing area and given vests and shorts to wear. Travis was bouncing around on his toes, he'd seen a movie about boxers and thought he knew it all. Ted took us to one of the soft mats.

"Now boys, I want to teach you to dance," he said smiling.

"Fuck off mate, we don't dance," Travis replied, skipping about and punching the air already breathless.

He chuckled and called over a guy to demonstrate.

"Mack, come over, show these girls here how it's done."

Mack looked to be mid twenties and fit. He had muscles on muscles and from his moves, he had been training as a boxer for some time. He showed us how to stand and keep the weight on the back foot. He showed us how to defend, the position of our arms and hands to deflect any punches and finally he showed us how to throw a punch.

We mucked about for a bit on the soft mats, Travis had seen Rocky, he knew what to do. We were not allowed to hit each other, but to stand apart and throw a soft punch to teach the other to block it. Before I knew it, a couple of hours had passed and Joe had returned. He was waving us over, it was time to go. I was disappointed, I could have stayed there all day. I had found something that I really enjoyed. Ted had said that we could come again and we looked at Joe in earnest. It was a dilemma, I would have gone every day but we still needed to earn money.

"You can come back tomorrow kid," he said, seeing the look on my face. "After you've run a couple of errands for me."

The following day the errands were much the same as we had done before. Drop off a package, collect the money and bring it back to Joe. We never asked what was in the packages, sometimes they were small, sometimes not. Travis had wanted to open one but I wouldn't let him. Some were wrapped in brown paper and some were boxes of kitchen items, toasters and such like. We had been trusted with a job and we had to get on with it. I had half an idea what we were delivering in the brown paper packages and I wasn't happy about it, but it was a way to survive. We took these deliveries to sleezy, run-down apartments and sometimes to big, large houses with long drives. Over a week we must have walked for miles. Often we would collect items from the office that Evelyn worked at, an import company I was told. It was always nice to see her and she would stop her work and make a point of chatting to us, checking we had eaten and we were clean. She fussed over us like I think a mother should have.

At one point she grabbed Travis by the collar and dragged him to the bathroom, dampening tissue she shoved it his ears while he squealed and tried to squirm away. I laughed until she stared, hard at me. I washed my own ears. There was a small bathroom in the office that we used but, according to Evelyn, not well enough.

****

We came close to getting picked up by the cops one day. I had a sense of being followed and without looking behind, I signalled to Travis to divert from the regular route we took. We scuttled down an alleyway and waited to see if I was right. I noticed a man in a blue jacket and jeans, one I had seen at various points throughout the day, stop at the top of the alley and stare down it, after us.

"Trav, keep walking, the cops are on to us," I told him.

"How do you know?" he said, turning to look back.

I grabbed his arm.

"Don't look, don't let him know we've seen him. That guy, I've seen him a few times today. I'm sure he's been following us," I said.

"You sure it's the cops? Wouldn't they have picked us up by now?" he asked.

It was a good point but I wasn't taking the chance either way. We carried on, the alleyway opened out onto an avenue running parallel and when we were clear of the corner we ran. I decided not to go to our drop off and not to return to Joe's either. I didn't want to lead anyone to either place. We hid out for a while in a local cafe, eating a pizza until I thought the coast was clear, then headed off to the gym.

"Ted, can you get a message to Joe?" I asked, as we entered.

"Sure kid, what's up?"

"I think we were being followed today, maybe the cops, I'm not sure, so I didn't make the drop. I didn't want to lead him back to Joe's, so I still have the package. Can you tell him that?" I asked.

He taped up our hands before he went off to make the call and Travis and I changed. Mack was working out with the heavy bag and once he saw us, he signalled for us to join him. He held the heavy bag and Travis went first, throwing a couple of punches. Mack would move the bag about making him move with it, sometimes lurching it forwards towards him.

When it was my time I squared up to it as I had been shown, my fists raised to my chin in defence and I hit that bag. When my fist connected, flashes of images would fire through my brain of every beating I took. I hit that bag as if I was defending myself back then. Nothing mattered to me than to punch and hurt. Every slap across the back with that belt, every minute of being preached to, every hour of chores, warranted a volley of punches to the bag in front of me. Sweat dripped from my forehead into my eyes, stinging and blurring my vision but still I carried on, hitting the bag with as much force as I could muster.

"Whoa kid, steady up," I heard.

I slowed the pace and Ted grabbed my wrists, inspecting my hands. Although he had put tape across them, blood seeped through from the grazes I had sustained to my knuckles. I looked down at them, in wonder. When had that happened? I felt no pain but an immense sense of release. Something triggered in my brain. I could hit out and it felt good, a small amount of years of pent up aggression was being set loose. Joe arrived at the gym and immediately called Travis and I over.

"What happened today kid?" he asked, while inspecting my fists.

I repeated what I had told Ted, about the man in the blue jacket and jeans, I was able to describe him well. I told Joe that I didn't think it wise to make the drop or return in case we brought whoever it was back to the office.

"You did good kid," was all he said. I handed him the package, grateful to be rid of it.

****

The days and weeks that followed were much the same. Instead of just running errands, we went to the gym as well. Travis and I were evenly matched on speed but I was stronger. All those years of sweeping and cutting logs meant I had muscular shoulders, a powerful punch for someone of my age. Soon enough we were able to get into the ring and spar, with each other and with Mack. Occasionally some of the other guys would challenge us, mocking and trying to rile us because of our age. Travis always bit, I just shook my head and out boxed them. We had fun, we learnt to fight and I learnt that I had found something I was very good at.

It took until my fifteenth birthday though, for me to be good enough to finally put Mack on the floor.

We had been sparring, Travis watching as I went a couple of rounds with Mack. We had gloves on and by now proper boots and shorts, bought with some of the money I had saved for us. Joe was watching, ringside with Ted. I could see them chatting, heads together and Ted shaking his at whatever Joe was saying.

For some reason that day I was pissed. I was getting restless with running errands, picking up laundry and shopping. I wanted to do something more challenging. I had been pestering Joe for a little while for Travis and I to do something else. I knew we were young but I thought we could handle a little more. Joe had said no, he wanted to keep us where we were. At the time I didn't understand his reasoning, we might have been fifteen but were much older in the head, more street wise than some of the older guys he had working for him.

I guess I wasn't concentrating when Mack threw a punch and it hit me square in the face. I felt my nose crack and a trickle of blood run down to my lips. I tasted it and something exploded in my head. I was immediately taken back to the days in Sterling. I did the total opposite to what was expected of me, I lowered my hands and I looked hard at Mack. Many years later, Mack would tell me that as my eyes got darker, the hairs on the back of his neck stood on end.

As he approached, I let out one punch, straight through his guard, square on his jaw and I watched in slow motion as he sailed backwards and landed with a thud on the mat. Ted jumped in the ring and grabbed my arms from behind. He was nowhere near strong enough to restrain me but somewhere in my angry brain I registered his voice and it stilled me.

"Kid, calm it down," I heard him say.

I tugged the string with my teeth to loosen my gloves, pulling them off and throwing them to the floor. I felt bad for Mack, he had been kind to me, we were only sparring and I had knocked him out cold. I walked over to where he lay and crouched down. I was expecting him to be angry, seriously angry with me. Instead, as he came round and was helped to his feet, still groggy, he gave me a soft punch to the head, a smile and I knew we were all right.

"Kid, you got anger issues," he said with a slur as Ted helped him out of the ring.

It was not an option going to the local hospital, too many questions would get asked, especially about where I lived, so Paul called over his wife, Rosa. She had been a nurse and she fixed my nose but it would always be crooked. Getting back to the office, Joe was regaling the guys of how I had outboxed Mack. Jonathan and Richard were there. I liked those guys, they showed Travis and I respect and bearing in mind they were so much older, they didn't have to do that. They treated us as one of the gang. The only person we didn't like was Joe's son, young Joey. He was about the same age as us but the total opposite. He was fat, weak and seemed to have a permanent sneer on his face. He was lazy. If he was sent on an errand it would take him all day, half the money spent on the way back and a fresh packet of cigarettes always in his top pocket.

****

"Come on, Joe, think about it," I said, one afternoon.

We had been having one of our regular conversations. I had asked to do more, I wanted to spend time with each of the guys, to understand what they did, helping and learning. He was having none of it. He wanted Travis and I there, with him. I got that he thought we were too young, he was becoming protective of us to a degree but I might have been fifteen in body but way older in the head.

"Jon, you think it's a good idea don't you?" I asked.

"Rob, you would be bored sitting with me all day, unless you're good with numbers," he replied.

"Come on, Richard, you need a hand, don't you? Joe, he can't collect all the rents on his own," I said.

Richard held up his hands in surrender, he wasn't getting involved in that debate.

Travis and I were relentless, every day nagging Joe until finally, a few months later, he gave in. He decided that we should spend some time with Richard first. Joe owned some property, there were rents to collect, repairs to be organised and we spent a week following Richard, watching and learning. When he thought we had learnt enough, we were given a block to ourselves.

"Travis, I want you to start on the top floor, Rob, you start on the bottom. It's rent day, knock on each door, collect the rent and whoever isn't in or doesn't pay, write it down," Richard said as he handed us each a small ring bound book.

The problem with Travis was that he thought he was God's gift to women and at fifteen, he certainly looked older. I had made it three quarters of the way up before Travis had got to his fourth flat. Every pretty lady that opened the door warranted a twenty minute chat. Travis would lean up against the wall flexing his muscles, giving them his killer smile and it always worked. I was amazed at how many ladies would stop and chat to him, flirting back. Until they saw me that was. They would finish their conversation quickly and close the door.

"You are my unlucky charm," Travis would moan, staring at the closed door of his favourite lady.

"Trav, she's old enough to be your mother," I replied. "And fucking ugly enough as well."

Unbeknown to me at first, the reason I got the bottom half of the block was because that was where most of the non payers were, by coincidence rather than on purpose. Richard told me later that day that he thought I looked intimidating enough to get results and I usually did. Sometimes I would come across some old, fat drunk in a string vest with nicotine stained hands. They would laugh as they opened the door, a kid sent to collect the rent. I would stand tall and quiet, listen to their rant and wait for their money. Other times it would be the mad cat woman. I don't think she understood that she had to pay her rent, if she wanted to live there. She always answered the door with a skinny, half eared cat in her arms, talking to it as if it could understand her.

"Mrs Wren, I've come to collect the rent," I would say, slowly and deliberately.

"What did he say?" she would ask the cat.

I would tap my foot impatiently waiting for the cat to answer her. However, it did seem to work. She would raise the cat to her ear and ask me if I was there to collect the rent. I often wished Mrs Wren would be out when I knocked.

By the time we had finished the block, Travis would have pocketed a couple of phone numbers and I would have all the money. Along with collecting the rent, we would have to listen to the tenants and their problems. The hot water wasn't hot enough, the kitchen tap wouldn't work, moaning about the amount of money they had to pay for the shit hole that they lived in. It was on the tip on my tongue sometimes to inform them that their apartment was way better than the back of a Chinese restaurant, where Travis and I had spent a year sleeping.

However, I took note of all their complaints and made sure the supervisor got the repairs done. I reasoned with Joe, if you repair what's broken, listen to their complaints, they seemed to pay their rent on time with no dodging us, and why shouldn't they have a tap that worked.

Each day followed the same pattern, we would shadow Richard, collecting rents from various buildings then head off to the gym for a session with Ted. Mack would be there and sometimes he would look like he had already been ten rounds with someone, and I often wondered exactly what he did for Joe.

****

Jonathan was the next person we worked with and he was wrong in that I didn't find what he did boring. Travis did, he was not good with numbers having never really been to school, but I soon got the idea of what was going on. The rents from the legitimate side of Joe's business went through the books. He paid tax on those to not draw any suspicion to the other money that seemed to wing its way back into the office.

"Is this drug money?" I asked outright, pointing to the stacks of notes I had seen in the safe.

"Some, Joe does a little dealing but no hard drugs, he doesn't like them," Jon replied.

"What's the difference? Drugs are drugs," I said.

I was not interested in drugs and to be honest, not best pleased to learn Travis and I had been the ones running those little packages all over the place.

"Kid, one thing you have to understand, people will always take drugs. Joe won't be involved in the hard stuff, just a little dope."

It was a burden to shoulder this knowledge, and yet I was proud that the information had been shared with us. Although only still young, we were obviously trusted members now.

"So, the money that you put through as rent is listed as being higher than is collected, you can then filter in the drug money. Would that mean paying more tax?" I asked.

Jonathan raised his eyebrows at me. "Smart kid, and yes it would, however what we have are many invoices and receipts to offset against any profits, bring the level of tax back down," he answered.

I found the whole thing interesting, Travis was bored and Jonathan amazed at my level of understanding the figures. We divided up some roles. Travis was left to obtain any invoices we may need, there were a couple of construction projects that Paul was involved in and he would provide what we wanted. I would log all the receipts, I had the neater handwriting after all and I booked in all the rent collected. It was my first lesson in basic book keeping.

There were things that we were not involved in, obviously. I would notice entries made or large wads of cash that were given to Jon to put in the safe and I knew better than to ask. There was a day, however, when the safe door was ajar, Jonathan having just popped out of the office.

“Look at all that money,” Travis had said. “One day we’re going to have that much.”

“One day we will, Trav. If we work hard, save, we’ll have a shit load ourselves.”

Earning money was becoming an obsession with me. I had filled my notebook and a further five by that time. I recorded what I earned, wrote down what I spent and each month would smile at the amount I had saved. I would have Jonathan check my figures and he would smile and nod, assuring me that mine and Travis’s cash was safe, ready for when we wanted it.

****

“Rob, I’ve brought you some lunch,” I heard behind me, one day.

Evelyn had come into the office, she had a rare day off. I had known her for nearly four years then and I still felt guilty about how we had first met.

She was not a tall woman, she only came up to my shoulders. She had the same dark brown hair and brown eyes as Joe. She was in her mid twenties. I had seen her out and about with a guy and I knew that Joe was unaware of this. It must have been hard for her to have grown up without her mother. She had told me her mother died and having an over protective Joe as a father, meant skulking around with any boyfriend she had. However, she was very keen for me to understand the man I had seen her with was just a friend, she didn’t want a boyfriend and I wondered why.

“Hi, Ev, I’m done here. Why don’t we get Trav and head outside?” I suggested.

As much as she was Joe’s daughter, I knew she didn’t like to be in that place. She kept her distance from her father’s choice of work. We found Travis and made our way outside, it was a bright sunny autumn day and we headed to the local park. It was not so much of a park, more a grassed area in the middle of apartment blocks, a couple of swings and a bench. Joe had paid for those to be put there, these were his apartment blocks and he wanted somewhere for the kids to play safely. Evelyn had made us sandwiches and we sat and ate, soaking up the sun.

“Rob, I’ve never asked, but how did you get to be here?” Evelyn said.

“To DC do you mean? Well, hitched a lift, hid in the back of a pickup, that kind of thing,” I said, knowing what she meant, but evading the question.

“You know what I mean,” she scolded.

I guess it wouldn’t hurt to finally tell them the truth. I trusted them both, they were family to me.

“I was born in London, as you know, and my parents died when I was six, I think. They were shit parents, never around, left me on my own most of the time, but one day they never came home. A car crash I was told. Anyway, I ended up in a foster home for a while before my dad’s sister came over from Pittsburgh to get me. Fucking right nutter she was. Spent her whole life at the church and beating or preaching at me. She thought everything that went wrong was my fault because I had the devil inside me,” I said.

I needed to take a pause, they knew what I had just said but not what was coming.

“When I was eleven, on my birthday that no one ever remembered, I took the belt she hit me with and the bibles, and set fire to them in the basement. The fire took hold and the house burnt down, with her in it. I killed her,” I said, noticing the shock registering on Evelyn’s face.

“You didn’t kill her, it was an accident wasn’t it? I doubt you could have done anything to save her, you were so young,” she said.

“No, that’s where you’re wrong. I watched that fire for a while, watched it take hold of the basement. I had plenty of chances to do something about it, but I didn’t. I had plenty of time to get her out of the house, but I didn’t. I stood at the edge of the woods and watched until there was nothing left of the house or her.”

“Man, that bitch deserved it,” Travis said. Whether he believed that or not it didn’t matter, he was always on my side.

Evelyn’s eyes were filled with pain and sadness. That was something I didn’t like to see, I didn’t want nor need pity from anyone. Brushing the crumbs from my lap, I stood.

"Anyway, it's all history now, we need to head back," I said.

"Did you stay around?" Evelyn asked as we made our way back towards the office.

"Only until the morning. I watched the priest and the cops kick through the embers, then I left. The rest you know," I said, with a shrug of my shoulders.

"Do the cops think you died in the fire?" Travis asked.

"I don't know. That's why I don't ever want to get picked up, Trav, but I doubt anyone is looking for me," I said, with a little sadness.

I still found it hard that Travis had no contact with any member of his family. I understood him wanting to get away. I knew what it was like to live a life of regular beatings but he had told me he had a sister he'd got on with. I had no family left, so the thought of him not wanting to know his, upset me a little.

"You should speak to dad about it," Evelyn said.

"Maybe, but right now, let's just keep it between us," I replied.

I would speak to Joe, one day, but it wasn't something I liked to just bring up. I was worried, if he knew that about me, he might send me packing.

****

Paul was the next person we were sent to work with. Travis was in his element and this time I found it all a little boring. There were a couple of building developments that Joe owned, he had wanted them to be more apartments. Apartments made more money than stores or commercial properties for Joe. We watched as Paul organised bribes to local government officials, to local businesses to support the development and to the unions to ensure the build was not disrupted by strikes. From what I could see, an awful amount of money was spent on getting the build through planning that might not have been necessary, had it gone down the regular channels anyway. At the end of the day, the buildings that Joe was developing were run-down, renovating them could only improve the area.

"Joe, I know you want to get the planning through quickly but why not try putting it through the normal channels first, then if it fails, grease a few palms. It just seems to me that we pay a lot of bribes when it might not be necessary," I said one day.

"Rob, we need these application to go through and quick," Paul had replied.

"I understand that, but do we really need to pay out money to the locals? I mean, let's be honest, they're not going to complain, are they? Fair enough, bride the unions if we have to but why the rest?" I said.

I wondered at times whether some of the bribe money found its way back into Paul's pocket. I just couldn't see the point of paying people to support a development that was going to enhance the area they lived in. New apartments meant more custom for the local stores and most of which Joe owned anyway.

To mine and Joe's amazement the second development sailed through with no opposition, saving a huge amount of money that would have automatically been paid out in bribes.

I don't think I was Paul's best friend that day. I came to realise that each of the guys that surrounded Joe, except for Jonathan, loved the notoriety that came with being associated with him. They loved the attention and the doors that opened because of that association. I wanted doors to open for me because they wanted to open for me and not because of who I knew. The only way for that to happen was to earn respect.

That started to come shortly after my sixteenth birthday. Travis and I were learning to drive, an essential if we were to continue to learn about the various pies Joe had his fingers in. As was the norm, we were at the gym after a day of working with Paul. Travis and I sparred regularly and to mix it up a little, some of the guys, including Mack, from the gym would challenge us. I was pleased that we both held our own. Joe had come to watch us and I noticed that familiar heads together conversation he was having with Ted. Instead of Ted's usual shake of the head, this time, they looked at me and he nodded.

"Kid, I have a proposition for you," Joe said, placing his arm around my shoulder.

"I have a fight coming up, it's against a twenty or something year old, don't know a lot about him and I wondered if you wanted the shot."

"You're asking me if I want to take part in a boxing match against someone no one knows anything about," I replied

"That about sums it up, but you should know, it's an unlicensed match," he answered.

"Sure, why not," I said.

"Kid, you have to understand what you're getting yourself into, before you agree," Ted butted in.

"Ted, I get it. I have to fight someone whilst Joe here, is going to have people bet. What's my percentage?" I asked, turning to him.

"Normally you would get a fee," he said.

"I'll tell you what, you need to get some people to bet on the other guy, make it a bit of a frenzy, stick me in as the outside bet and I'll take a quarter of what you earn," I said.

"The kid's learning," Joe said to Ted, a proudness creeping into his voice.

"Rob, you don't have to do this," Travis told me later that night.

"Do what?" I asked.

"The boxing. If no one knows anything about your opponent how can you prepare?"

"It's just a boxing match, Trav. No one knows anything about me so we're evenly matched," I said.

We were still sleeping in the office on our makeshift beds, the lights were off but I would not allow the blinds to be pulled. I liked to feel that I was part of the outdoors. I hated confined spaces and being able to see the stars and the moon made me feel comfortable and safe.

"Listen, Trav. I'll never do anything I don't want to, trust me on that, but we can earn some serious money. You know I'll split with you and we can buy ourselves a car soon."

Every dime I earned was either saved or spent on essentials only. We had quite a little stash of money of our own sitting in the safe in Joe's office. Another reason Travis and I were quite happy to sleep there overnight, to guard our savings.

For the next couple of weeks I trained even harder than I had before. I already knew how to box I now needed to know if I had the stamina to last the distance. I worked out on the treadmills, the weight machines and with the help of Ted and Mack, I boxed like my life depended on it. I still got that sense of satisfaction when I hit someone, that release of pent up aggression and anger and I enjoyed it. I enjoyed seeing the blood spurt when I connected with someone's eye or nose. When the day of the fight arrived Evelyn came to see me.

"I don't want you to do this, Rob," she said, worried for me. I was, after all, only sixteen.

"Ev, no one can hurt me. They might break my skin, my bones but no one will ever hurt me inside," I replied.

"That's not the point, Rob. You're getting too involved in the business, I worry about you both."

She was right, for the past few months Travis and I were getting increasingly involved, with that came knowledge of what Joe did. That could be dangerous for us but without realising it, I got addicted to it, to the money and to the new found respect that was shown to me.

It was that respect that I craved, never having had it before. No one had cared about me until then. The kids at school had sniggered at me, my aunt hated me for what she thought I represented and now at sixteen, I was bigger, stronger than some adults. Although I did not confuse some people's fear of me with respect, I thrived on both.

We arrived later that night at a disused warehouse, on the outskirts of town. There were cars parked everywhere. Ted carried my bag and with me were Joe, Travis and Mack. Joe already had men inside, altering the betting, making me the outside bet. Paul, Richard and Jonathan were in the crowd, there to support me. I changed and warmed up in a small room. Ted fixed my hands and pulling on the gloves, I was ready for my first fight.

"Are you sure about this, Rob? Are you nervous?" Travis asked me.

I thought for a moment. "No," I said and I wasn't, I didn't feel any nerves at all, maybe that was wrong.

I entered the room, there was a ring and a referee in the middle and as I waited to be announced, I noticed a guy enter from the opposite direction. He looked to be a little bigger, a little taller but it was difficult to tell.

We walked towards the ring at the same time, Ted held the ropes so I could climb in. I watched my opponent dance around, throw some punches in the air. This gave me time to study him and to see how he fought. I would often wonder why they did that. I could get the measure of my opponent at that moment, judge the speed at which they threw a punch. I did none of that, not wanting to give anything away. Instead I stood rock still and watched him.

The referee called us together, they had the same rules as a licensed fight, it ended after twelve rounds or until one was unable to continue. All the time he danced around, hyped up, perhaps on something he shouldn't have been. I stared at him, looking directly at his eyes, reading him and was pleased to see that he struggled to hold my gaze. I could see apprehension in his eyes.

The referee pushed us apart, the bell sounded and this time I moved, keeping just out of his reach, watching every move he made. He seemed a little worried about throwing a punch, his eyes darting around, not wanting to connect with me.

I had intimidated him and right from the off put him on the back foot, so to speak. My hands kept up by my face, looking for the moment and still I waited for him to throw his first punch. People were calling out, cheering, but I emptied my mind of everything around me, just concentrated on the task in hand. Soon enough I heard nothing, just the rush of blood around my head and my heart steadily beating in my chest.

I had him worried, I was totally unknown. He threw his first punch and I deflected it easily, he followed this with one to my side, I didn't flinch. I felt no pain, as if the contact hadn't happened. If that was all he had got then this was going to be easy. He let go with another couple of punches, one to the side of my head, it didn't even rock me from my position. Now he looked scared, his eyes were darting to his corner. He followed with more punches to my head and I kept coming forwards, forcing him back towards to ropes.

It was my turn now, I had given him enough time to learn all I could from him. As quick as a flash my arm swung out, connecting with his jaw, around the side of his gloves. My first punch and he rocked back on his feet for a moment. However, the bell saved him, round one over.

I gently strolled to my corner and Ted sat me down.

"Good going kid, but people have come to watch a fight, you know, bloodshed and all that," he said.

"I'm watching what he's got, learning how he moves," I replied.

The bell sounded for the second round and I walked to the middle of the ring, watched him bounce on his toes and what was more important, I saw the confidence seep out of him. A slow smile crept on my face. I had the measure of him and now I knew exactly what I was going to do, how this was going to end.

My first punch connected straight between his gloves, his defence not good enough to stop the blow. His nose broke, blood splattered across my face and that something triggered in my head again. In my mind, I felt a blow across my back, a buckle biting into my skin and I punched repeatedly, forcing him back on the ropes. I didn't want him on the floor, I wanted to hit him over and over. My breath hadn't even quickened, my heart a steady rate and then I finally saw him. His crumpled face was bloodied, his hands hung down by his sides with no attempt to protect himself and I stopped. I took a step back and watched him fall to the floor. The referee stood over him waving his arms, game over and his corner jumped in the ring, rushing to him.

I had done that. I had bloodied that man's face, broke his nose, his jaw and who knows what else. I looked down at my chest, covered in his blood and yet I felt nothing. I could hear the screaming of the crowd, a pack of wolves howling my name and I stood and looked coldly at them. They disgusted me. I watched the people closest to the ring shrink back a little. It was the women I noticed the most. The ones draped in fur coats and jewels, hanging off an arm of older guys in suits, most smoking cigars. Some blew kisses, their coats falling open to reveal skimpy outfits. I saw Jonathan but he didn't smile, high five like the others had done, he just looked at me and I saw a sadness in his eyes.

I felt arms around me, pulling me to my corner.

"Come on kid," Ted said.

He undid my gloves, pulling them off. Joe and Travis jumped in the ring to congratulate me. I walked across to the other corner where the guy was sitting on his chair. His team tried to protect him, not sure what my motive was but I pushed through them and crouched down to face him. He looked at me, a beaten man, a faint smile from his bruised and split lips. He nodded just the once but that was all I needed, forgiveness for what I had just done. I left that building with not a scratch on me and a huge wad of money in my pocket.

"You all right kid?" Ted asked on the journey home.

I had been silent in the car, leaving Travis and Joe excitedly reliving, second by second, the short fight and I looked across at Ted in the dark of the car.

"Ted, I took no pleasure from that, I did it for the money, that's all," I said.

He nodded to me, he understood.

I learnt a lesson that night. I learnt that I had to control every aspect of me, tightly. I was capable of causing real harm to someone but what scared me most was I felt nothing about what I had done. Not joy in winning my first fight, not pleasure in probably leaving that man with scars and equally, I felt no remorse either. I was just empty of any emotion.

Instead of going back to the office we went straight to Joe's, Evelyn anxiously paced the driveway when she saw the car pull in. She ran straight to me, checking for any cuts or bruises.

"Are you okay, Rob?" she asked.

I nodded, smiled at her for reassurance. "I'm fine, Ev, it was easy," I replied.

"Did you win?" she asked.

"Of course he won, look at him. Let me tell you how it went down," Travis said, placing his arm around her shoulder and walking her into the house, detailing the fight.

We stayed at the house that night. Travis and I shared a room with twin beds and after listening to him talk constantly about the fight, he drifted off to sleep. I lay there, eyes wide open thinking about what I had done. I knew I would fight again, that wouldn't be the one and only, but I had decided I would not make it a regular thing, I would not end up like that guy. His only purpose in life was to fight to earn someone else money. No doubt he had no choice in the matter. Now he would be thrown to one side, his usefulness ended. He would have earned from the fight, I just hoped it was enough to have been worth it.

I was not dumb, I knew the guys that took part in these fights had a Joe behind them, someone who pulled their strings. Some had no choice, they were indebted to their Joe and I vowed I would not be like that. I owed no one, I would never be indebted to anyone. I earned my money and I looked on Joe like a father. I knew he was different, he would not force me to do anything I didn't want to.

****

The following morning I woke to the smell of breakfast, Evelyn and her sister Maria were in the kitchen. Maria was younger, an odd person, always quiet and perhaps more affected by her mother's death than the others. Travis and I headed downstairs, Joe was already sitting at the table and waved us over.

"You did great last night, Rob," he said.

"Thanks, but I have to be honest, I didn't get any pleasure from it," I replied.

He nodded, deep in thought.

"If you want, there's another fight in a month's time, someone a little tougher but it will be entirely your decision," he said, taking a mouthful of food. "You've certainly got some attention though."

I put down my fork. "Joe, I didn't feel anything, not joy, not remorse, nothing," I said.

He stilled, thinking, a sad smile crossed his lips and he patted my shoulder, his way of comforting me.

"One day that might be a help to you," was all he said.

We continued with our breakfast, again Travis telling Evelyn about the fight, blow by blow, asking Joe if he could get one.

****

For the next few weeks I trained, we went to work and we continued to learn to drive. Without really taking any kind of test, we were handed our permits and Travis crashed the first car we were allowed out in on our own. For a while I refused to get in another with him, he was a liability, a speed freak. One day, though, we ended up in a chase, the cops had seen him speeding and there was no way I wanted to get caught. This time I encouraged Travis to speed up, dodge in and out of the traffic and lose them, which he eventually did. It unnerved me though. Arriving back at the office, I needed to talk to Joe, alone.

“Joe, I need to speak with you,” I said.

He looked up from some papers he was working on, gesturing for me to take a seat. I glanced around at the other guys who got the hint and left us to it.

“What’s up kid?” he asked.

“I need to know, if the police ever pick me up, whether I can get charged with murder or not.”

He looked at me, eyes wide in shock at what I had just said. “Go on,” he encouraged.

I told him about my life, my parents and how I ended up in America. I watched his eyes widen with disgust as I spoke about my aunt.

“I killed her and I need to know, if the police ever pick me up will they know that.”

“Did anyone see you do it?” he asked, his mind already thinking.

“No, I ran, hid in the woods until the morning then I left for here.”

“So if no one saw you, there is nothing to say you hadn’t run away before a batty old woman set fire to her house by accident, is there?” he replied.

“Did anyone know she beat you?” he asked.

“Yeah, the local priest, he encouraged her. They thought I had the devil in me,” I chuckled.

“He did what?” he asked, his eyes even wider, his hands slamming down on the table. Joe hated any abuse of children.

“He encouraged her. They thought if they beat me enough they could cleanse me, get the devil out, I guess.”

Although I hadn’t seen him go to church, the fact a priest was involved made him even angrier. His face reddened, I could see the veins in his neck bulge. He took a deep breath, as if to calm himself.

"Where was this?" he asked as he picked up his pen.

I told him where I had lived, the name of the Father and the school. I didn't ask why he wanted to know but I had an idea.

"Joe, one day I'll visit the Father."

He looked at me for a long while before he said, "Rob, learn one lesson from me. You don't serve your own justice, you order someone else to."

I wasn't entirely sure what he meant at the time. Many years later however, I understood. That statement was the start of a very different path for me. Joe had plans for my future, I guess he saw something in me at that young age to know I would be his successor.

"Who else knows?" he asked.

"Just Travis and Ev," I told him.

"Let's keep it that way. I'll ask around but my guess is that you're in the clear. If anyone asks, I'll tell them that you came here earlier than you did. You deny any knowledge of it, you ran to get away from her and she was alive and kicking when you did. Okay?"

I nodded my thanks and left to get on with my job. Joe had wanted me to collect a debt that was owed. He didn't anticipate any trouble and after my fight, word had already got round I was not someone to tangle with. I would use that to my advantage. The debt we were to collect was from a guy who had borrowed a lot of money. He had paid most of it back but had decided he had done enough and was holding on to the last of it. I didn't care whether he thought he had the right. He had paid a great deal of interest, I knew that, but he had been lent the money in good faith and whether he was morally right or wrong, the debt needed to be cleared.

We arrived at the store the guy owned and watched for a little while outside, waiting for it to clear of customers. It was just a convenience store, like everything else in the neighbourhood, tatty and run-down. Entering, Travis pulled the door shut behind us and turned over the open sign, indicating that the store was closed, he slid across the bolt.

"What the fuck do you think you're doing?" a voice shouted.

A grubby, fat man sat on a stool behind the counter, his greasy hair stuck to his forehead. The front of his torn T-shirt stained with whatever he had eaten for lunch. At his shout his friend appeared from a behind a door, a storeroom I guessed.

"I'm here to collect your last payment to Mr. Morietti," I asked, politely.

The man laughed, coughing up phlegm which he spat on the dusty floor at my feet. I looked down at it in disgust.

"Get this, that prick Joe, sent two kids to collect his money," he laughed again, his friend joining in.

"What the fuck you gonna do kid, beat me up," he said, finding this highly amusing.

I stood rock still, my eyes boring into him and I watched a flicker of uncertainty as he swallowed hard, his bravado wavering. The only people who referred to Joe by that name were the people closest to him. That man had just seriously disrespected him. Travis took a step closer to me, there was a glance between us, a flick of his eyes, a silent communication of what we were going to do and both men noticed this.

"I don't have his money," he said, trying to keep his voice calm.

Out of the corner of my eye I noticed the guy by the storeroom door reach inside his jacket. Before he could get to whatever it was, Travis was onto him. He punched him repeatedly. The guy didn't see it coming and he went down like a sack of spuds, crumpled on the floor and out cold. I never took my eyes off the one behind the counter who now looked in shock at his friend.

"I've come to collect what you owe," I said quietly and I watched him, with trembling hands, open his till and take out a wad of cash.

As he handed it over I grabbed his wrist, pulled him forwards so he was half over the counter and I leant my face close enough to smell the stench of him.

"If you ever disrespect me or Mr. Morietti in that way again, I will break every bone in your fucking hands. You will never work again, you will struggle to even wipe that filthy ass of yours. Do you understand?" I said.

He nodded, I hoped his fear had made his mouth too dry to speak.

"I said, do you understand?" I growled.

"Yes, yes I understand, now take the money," he replied.

We left, checking the coast was clear, started up the car and drove off. Travis laughed, he found everything funny, even beating the shit out of someone amused him. I didn't know who was worse, him for liking to fight or me for not have any emotion one way or another about it. Shaking my head at him, I told him to gun it, let's get the payment back to Joe then we can hit the gym. When we got back to the office Joey was there. Neither me nor Travis had taken to him, we tended to avoid each other as much as possible and the feeling was mutual.

"Joe around?" I asked.

"No. What can I do for you, Rob?" he asked, spitting my name.

"I have some money for him, that's all. I'll catch up with him later," I replied and as we turned to leave, he said, "Give to me, I'll deal with it."

"It's cool, Joey. I'll wait until I see Joe," I replied, the tension between us mounting.

"I said, give it to me."

There was no way I was going to give him the money. I doubted all of it would find its way back to Joe and I would be accountable for the rest. I turned to leave and felt a hand grip my arm. I stopped and looked down at it.

"Joey, do yourself a favour, take your fucking hand off me," I said, in a low growl.

His hand shook a little. "You need to watch yourself, Rob," he said.

I spun round so fast he stumbled back a little. Travis lounged against the desk with a smirk on his face.

"From who, Joey? You?" I said, staring at him, watching him shrink before me.

I laughed, nodded at Travis and without a backward glance we left the office. I knew I had made an enemy that day, I had no idea to what extent and how that would affect me later in my life.

****

I guessed Travis and I were fearsome. We noticed that when we walked along the sidewalk people would either move out of our way or greet us with a tentative handshake. People recognised and respected us, girls threw themselves at us.

Travis was the first to get laid, it was with a married woman, someone we collected rent from and he was also the first to get caught. I remembered the day. He came running down the apartment stairwell, laughing and clutching his clothes to his chest. A man, way older, was running after him, cursing. I stood and watched Travis run to the car, jump in and wheel spin away. He had his middle finger out the window to the guy who was, by then, bent double, hands on his knees, wheezing like mad.

"For fuck's sake, Travis, not on our bloody doorstep," I cursed, quietly, at him.

I watched the man rise, mumble and as he turned to return to his apartment, he saw me. He stilled, unsure of what to do. He knew of me, he knew Travis and I worked together.

I shook my head in exasperation. "I'll have a word with him," I said as I passed.

I often had to clear up one mess or another Travis had got into and I started to walk back to the office.

My first sexual encounter was in a club one night that Joe owned. Travis and I had just discovered the delights of beer and clubs. Although not old enough to gain entry, let alone buy a beer, because of who we were, we were allowed in. We would get dressed up and had a place reserved for us by the bar. We would go there on a Friday after the gym, leaving in the early hours of the Saturday morning.

At first the small group of girls were annoying, so transparent, giggling, making sure they stood as close to us as possible to order their drinks. We would pick a couple out, fuck them in the toilets or out back against the wall then come back for another. It was quick and without any real feeling. They were cheap and easy and I had no respect for any of them. It was hard to have the respect, these girls would join their friends knowing they had all been fucked by us and compare their experience.

Neither me or Travis had any trouble picking up girls, they saw us, saw the lifestyle we lived, the money we earned and they would assume we were older. The only problem was that they always wanted something neither of us were willing to give, a relationship. I doubted we would know how to have one, let alone take a girl out, wine and dine them. It wasn't necessary, we got what we wanted without the expense.

I guess like any teenager with raging hormones, I loved sex, I fucked a lot. I took what I wanted without any real thought to giving pleasure. Part of the problem was that I didn't like these girls, I had no desire to please them. All I wanted was my release. I must have been doing something right though, the girls lined themselves up for me.

****

"Trav, do you want a fight?" Joe had asked one day.

"Sure thing, what have you got?" he replied.

"A young kid, done well so far, not lost a fight, might not be easy," he warned.

So Travis prepared for his first fight. It was to be held on the same night as my next one. We trained together, prepared and as a surprise Ted had some new matching shorts made for us, in the club colours.

We arrived at the venue, the usual disused warehouse, often one Joe owned. It would always be kept secret until the last minute for fear of the cops closing it down. They were starting to get a bit heavy on illegal gambling, often raiding the place just before the fight started. We found our makeshift changing room and readied ourselves. I wanted to watch Travis, it was his first fight so we headed out, ringside.

As Travis entered the ring I saw his opponent, maybe mid twenties, already a broken nose, a seasoned fighter. I also noticed something odd about his gloves, they didn't seem to have the shine they would normally have. It was an old trick, paint on some glue and dip the gloves in crushed glass or sand to cause more damage to the skin when they connected. I whispered to Ted, he had to let Travis know so that he was aware. I cursed that the ref had not picked up on it, or maybe he had and chose to do nothing about it.

The bell sounded for round one. Travis was far more impulsive than me, he steamed straight in throwing punches. He didn't take the time to watch his opposition, to learn how he would move or respond and he soon found himself on his ass from an uppercut that he had not seen coming.

It's not like he was hurt, more surprised, but it was an introduction to his negligence. Round two saw a slightly more cautious Travis, he backed off a little but he had grazes to his face from the roughed up gloves. Now, there was something Travis was obsessed about, his looks. When he realised his face was marked, he got pissed, really pissed. Being angry in a boxing ring is not always the best thing, it makes you careless. For the second time, he ended up on the floor. At the end of round two I climbed to the ropes and leant over his shoulder.

"What the fuck are you doing, Trav?" I asked.

He looked round at me.

"Back off bro, watch what he's doing then wait for your moment, keep away from the gloves, they've done something to them," I said.

In the meantime the betting was going mad, a win for the other guy and if Travis didn't alter what he was doing, they would be right.

The bell sounded for round three and the guys squared up to each other. If Travis got his head together, they would be evenly matched but he was allowing his emotions to distract him. Joe and Ted were looking worried, there was a lot of money riding on Travis winning. People around the ring were starting to mock him. I began to get angry, he was seventeen for fuck's sake. I started to shout at Travis to pick up the pace and finally he began to box the way I knew he could. He lasted the whole match but lost on points and he was devastated. I put my arm around him, led him back to the changing room, not before watching his opponents corner laugh at him and not before shouting at a group of guys who mocked him as we passed, happy to see them back off in fear.

My turn and I was angry, I wanted revenge. The guy I was to fight had the same corner team. Like Joe, they were fielding two fighters and like the previous gloves, these ones were altered to cause as much damage as possible. I squared up to my guy, my heart pounding, not in fear but in preparation for what I was about to do.

The bell sounded and I backed right off, moving around the ring, watching for any weakness. He was an arrogant bastard, taunting me, trying to rile me.

“I fucked your momma last night,” he said.

“Bet that was pleasant, she’s been dead ten years,” I replied.

Unlike Travis, I could be very angry and internalise it until it was time to let it out. A straight punch through his defence caused him to stumble backwards, opening his hands slightly. I saw my opportunity and I let rip, he didn’t stand a chance. I didn’t care that the crowd wanted to see a fight, this would be over in round one. These guys had come to this fight and cheated, that was something I would not let go. Fair enough, Travis was outboxed, but to doctor the gloves was wrong.

A volley of punches hit the guy on the head, the face, his stomach and his knees buckled. He might have been a good fighter but I had speed on my side and I would not give him a chance to get even the most feeble of punches thrown my way. I had him on the ropes and all he could do was to keep his gloves up to his face. I was too close for him to do anything to me. My last punch was the hardest I had ever thrown, an uppercut. I heard a crack and his arms instantly fell to his sides. I watched his eyes roll back in his head before he had even hit the floor. He never got up. I stood over him, watching the panic in his teams faces. As I approached them, they backed away leaving their guy lying in the middle of the ring and the crowd quietened.

“You did that,” I shouted in their faces, pointing at him.

“You roughed up those gloves and that is what happens when you fuck with me,” I told them.

I pushed past the ref as he tried to calm me down, climbed under the ropes and made my way out, leaving a room full of silenced spectators. Travis and Ted ran to keep up. We changed back into our clothes and headed out for the car. I was pumped, I bounced on my toes unable to keep still. Joe, with Mack by his side had the shirt of the referee bunched in his fist. As he saw us approach he pushed the ref away and we climbed in the car.

We arrived back at the house and sitting in the kitchen while Evelyn cleaned up Travis's face, I turned to Joe.

"Did you know about the gloves?" I asked, not taking my eyes from him.

"Rob, of course not. I know it happens, but I expected a fair fight, same as you two," he said. "The ref knew and he'll pay for that, don't you worry."

Joe had lost a lot of money on Travis that night but that was the risk he had taken.

"Set him up another fight, soon as," I told Joe, before heading off to bed.

****

As the months wore on, we stayed more and more with Joe, abandoning our little camp at the office. Joey and we still danced around each other, still avoided any real contact but I had started to feel a huge resentment from him. He'd had his opportunities, no different to Travis and I but he chose to not take them, to rely on his father for handouts instead of earning his own money.

Travis got his second fight and this time he won, easily. We fought on average, once a month earning big bucks towards the end. We had many offers to travel for fights, they could be arranged in New York and even Vegas for much more money than we had earned so far. As much as I told Travis to go for it, if he wanted to, it wasn't for me. Joe had enough guys at the club to do that.

"It has been put to me that you two should fight each other," Joe said one morning.

"What do you mean?" Travis asked.

"An associate let's call him, in New York, asked to put the pair of you in the ring. I told him no but it's only right you make the decision," he said.

"No, I won't fight my brother," I replied.

"How much?" Travis asked.

"A lot, big money," Joe replied.

"It's still a no," I said again, scowling at Travis for even being mildly tempted.

Travis and I looked at each other then back at Joe with a shake of our heads. We were brothers, we would never get in the ring against one another for real. I believed I would win, no doubt Travis thought the same, but I wouldn't fight him. I would spar with him, I had an element of control when it was just for fun or training, but in that ring, with those spectators calling out my name, I didn't trust myself not to hurt him.

****

One day we were called into the office, Joe wanted a job done. A lorry load of cigarettes would take an unfortunate detour. We would relieve the driver of his cargo, he would wait a couple of hours before calling the cops and reporting the robbery. Both the driver and Joe would earn well from this. Sometimes the lorries would be full of booze, other times it would be household items. What we were to do with a lorry load of kettles and toasters amused Travis and I for a long time.

We arrived at the office to collect a package, it should contain the money required to ensure the driver would have amnesia. Pushing open the door, I noticed Joey sitting in his father's chair, his feet resting on the desk.

"Where's Joe?" I asked, no attempt at politeness anymore.

"Out, money's there," he replied, pointing to a bundle wrapped in brown paper.

After picking this up Travis and I made our way outside, into our car and headed off.

"Trav, pull over, something isn't right," I told him.

Instead of going to the warehouse, Travis drove to an underground parking lot and taking a small penknife from my pocket, I pierced a small hole. Withdrawing the knife, I noticed a white powder on the end. Cocaine, I guessed. What had raised my suspicion was that money was not normally wrapped in brown paper, drugs were. In the past Joe would give the money in an envelope and I knew he was not involved in hard drugs, a little dope was all he would tolerate. Getting out of the car, I hid the package and we headed off to the meet.

Arriving at a warehouse, similar to the places we boxed at and where the lorry should have been in the process of being unloaded, my suspicions were confirmed. There was no lorry to be seen, however, the door was slightly open. We made the one and only mistake we have ever made that day.

We parked the car and got out, made our way through the door into the dark room. A look passed between Travis and I, a silent message to stay quiet. We separated up, each moving to one side of the building, my instincts and hearing on high alert. I heard them and I calculated there to be about three people but they were heading Travis's way. He was out of sight, no way for me to communicate with him without giving away both our locations.

"What the fuck?" I heard him say as he was grabbed from behind.

I stood in the shadows. It was not that I hadn't wanted to get to Travis as quick as possible but I needed to see who they were, what they were up to. I caught the glint of something shiny, where the moonlight had filtered through the broken windows. Someone held a knife to Travis's throat. This was serious and I had to make a plan and quickly.

"Where is it?" someone asked.

"What? Where the fuck is what?" Travis replied.

"My coke you prick. What do you think you should have brought here?" came an answer.

I was able to judge the whereabouts of everyone in the room by where their voices were coming from.

"Where's your boyfriend?" another asked, laughing. I thought I recognised the voice but just couldn't place from where. The voice was slightly distorted by the cavernous room.

"Come on out, Robert, hiding like the fucking rat you are," he shouted, his voice echoing around the empty space.

I stayed in the shadows against the wall, moving silently and feeling my way around the building until I was on the same side as them. I heard a rattle, it sounded like a chain of some sort and then a thud and I could just make out Travis on the floor. The chain had been swung, catching his legs and knocking him off balance. As my eyes adjusted to the dim light I watched as someone bent down, pulled Travis's head up by his hair and punched him, splitting his lip. Travis laughed, spitting the blood on the floor at the feet of his captor. He would have been more than capable of taking on at least two of them, had they not jumped him first.

"Call for your friend," I heard being said. Travis would not utter a word.

I was getting close, instead of three, there were four men. One was bent close to Travis, a second holding the end of the chain that was still wrapped around his legs. I could also see his hands bound behind his back and he was lying on his side, still with that stupid smile on his face. I watched as two other guys separated off and made their way around the room. As they moved through the areas lit by the moon, I could make out objects glinting in their hands, one had a gun, the other a knife. They knew I was there, Travis and I never travelled without each other but they had no idea exactly where I was. I had the advantage though, the ability to be quiet, to move silently. I had to take out these two guys without being shot at, stabbed and without being noticed.

Travis and I never carried weapons as such, just the odd knife. Until then our fists and our reputations were all we needed to get whatever job done that was necessary. This was something else though. I slowed my breathing and concentrated on the task in front of me. As much as I loved Travis, he was my brother, I had to focus on what was needed, even after I heard him scream. I knew they were using Travis to draw me out, but if he was to live, if both of us were to live, I needed to take out the two guys moving around the warehouse first.

I had no doubt the intention was to cause us serious harm, if not kill us and I also knew this had nothing to do with a lorry load of cigarettes or a kilo of coke. We had been set up and I had a strong suspicion who had organised it.

My foot gently touched something on the floor, a piece of rope, now I had my weapon. I silently made my way up behind the guy with the knife, he was the closest and had made a huge mistake.

He had moved too far into the shadows and behind a stack of wooden crates, out of sight of his friend and too far away to be saved. I took off my jacket and very quietly let it fall just behind him. As I wrapped the rope around his fat neck, his hand flew to his throat. He had no idea just how close behind him I had been.

I tightened the rope, crossing it over at the back of his neck, pulling it. I had not said a word and fortunately the only sound the guy could make was a soft gurgling as I, eventually, crushed his windpipe, killing him. It took a little longer than I'd expected and before he stilled, he managed to swipe his arm back, his knife connecting with my side. I heard it slice through my skin and I felt the hot blood run down, but there had been no pain.

Once he stilled I let him gently fall to the floor, the knife landing on my jacket, dulling any noise of it hitting the concrete. I picked up the knife and turned in the opposite direction, towards the second one. As hard as it was, I tuned out the sound of Travis. I had no idea what they were doing to him but he would keep making an angry scream. It was not one of fright, just pain and in between I could hear him laugh, swearing at the men holding him.

"Is that all you got, you fat fucker? Bring it on," he would shout. I knew what he was doing, he would shout allowing me to move faster, his voice covering any sounds I made.

"Rob, show yourself and poor Travis here might just keep his bollocks," I heard.

No one called me Rob other than Joe or his team. I was now confident in knowing exactly who had set us up.

A little way ahead of me was a tall guy, skinny and even from where I was, I could see the hand that held the gun already shaking with fear. I crept up behind him, caught him by the hair and turned him around. He made to shout but before he could, I shoved the knife in his chest to the hilt and his eyes grew wide with shock. The gun crashed to the floor, the noise it made echoing around the room.

"Lou, where are you?" someone shouted and I detected a little panic in his voice. It was the one who was crouched on the floor next to Travis. I made my way around the room again, keeping to the walls where it was darkest but not before picking up the gun.

I needed to stay in the shadows. If they had had any sense they would have taken Travis to the middle of the room where it was bathed with moonlight, forcing me to show myself. But they were stupid, they clearly hadn't thought this through. They had organised this 'attack' about as good as a group of school kids. By staying where they were, they allowed me to get close enough to be able to raise the gun with a direct easy shot.

I had never fired a gun before, although I'd held plenty, they were always lying around the office. I instinctively knew I had a good aim and I would pull that trigger if I had to. I had already checked to see if there was a safety catch, finding none, I placed my finger on the trigger and stepped into view.

Travis was on his back, his hands tied behind him, his legs bound together with a piece of chain and the front of his shirt covered in blood. There were cuts to the whole of his stomach and chest, not deep enough to kill him, just enough to make him scream out. His face was a mess. Boy, he was going to be pissed when he saw himself. One eye was already closed and his lip split and bleeding.

"Rob, these pricks here want to have a friendly chat with you," Travis laughed, spitting more blood on the floor.

I glanced quickly at him and gave him a nod. My focus was then on the guy with the chain, with a knife in his hand, the one who had hurt my brother. I slowly walked towards him. I saw him tremble and the fear was evident in his eyes. He hadn't banked on this, on me taking out two of his friends, then coming for him.

The fat bloke stood, now I knew exactly who he was. The grease ball from the store, the one who hadn't wanted to pay his last payment, and the one holding Travis, the same guy he had decked that day. I shook my head in amusement, a smile creeping across my lips. I watched them look from one to another.

"Tut, tut. You have both made a very big mistake today," I said.

"Lou," he shouted.

"Lou isn't coming, neither is the other one. If I let you live, you will find one dead over there and one dead that side," I indicated with my head.

“Now, you,” I pointed the gun at the one with the knife. “You are going to help my friend up from the floor, you’ve already ruined his clothes.”

He looked to his friend for support.

“Now,” I shouted and he startled.

He unwrapped the chain from Travis’s legs.

“Cut his hands free and if you so much as make the tiniest nick, this bullet will very quickly rip straight through your fucking brain,” I growled.

I couldn’t remember a time I had ever felt so angry and every time I looked at my blood stained brother, the anger intensified. He did as he was told. Travis rubbed some circulation back in his hands then as quick as flash he grabbed the man’s wrist, snapped it back and snatching the knife from his hand, he plunged it in his throat. He made an awful noise, blood spurted from his neck and his legs crumbled beneath him. That left the fat grease ball, quivering, still on his knees with tears and snot running down his face. I crouched down in front of him.

“I know who sent you, but I want to hear it from your fucking mouth,” I said

He shook his head.

“Right now, who are you more afraid of?” I asked. “Because it should be me.”

He looked up at me, my eyes would have displayed my anger and he shrunk away. He scrabbled with his hands to get himself as far away as possible until he hit the wall, nowhere left to go. I placed the muzzle of the gun against one knee cap as a reminder that I wanted an answer.

“It wasn’t supposed to happen like this,” he whimpered.

“What, you were only supposed to frighten us? Is that what you’re saying?” I said.

“No,” he answered

“So, you intended to what, kill us?” I asked, amazed at his stupidity.

He nodded.

“I will ask you one last time, who sent you?” I said, my face so close to his.

“Joey,” he whispered.

“Joey sent you, a group of fucking clowns to kill us, and you seriously thought you could do that?” I was amazed.

Still, it was confirmation of what I already knew. For the fee of a kilo of cocaine, Joey had hired this bunch of fuck wits to kill us. I laughed then, what planet was he on? These people, Joey, no one scared me. I would have to have emotion to be scared, that feature of being human had been long buried. The only thing I ever felt was anger. As Joe had once told me, to feel no emotion would help me one day, that day it had.

“I’m going to let you live, you prick, but everyone is going to know you fucked with us,” I said as I stood and took a step back.

I took the knife that was still embedded in the throat of his friend and holding the grease balls head I made a cut, deep and through his eyebrow.

“Every time you look in the mirror, you’ll see that scar and you’ll remember this day, you will remember me. I will watch you for the rest of your life and one day, when you least expect it, when you think I’ve forgotten you, I will be back,” I said.

Before we left, I stamped my foot as hard as I could, breaking one ankle then the other. Travis came over, he did the same to his hands, crushing as many bones as he could and the exertion from our punishment caused our wounds to bleed more. I punched his face, breaking his nose. Travis kicked him repeatedly, breaking his ribs and with the fat pig curled up in a ball trying to protect himself, I spat on him, like he had tried to do to me. The ultimate insult in my eyes. Using my shirt I cleaned the gun of any prints and wrapped the hand of the fat fucker around it, insurance for another time.

I helped Travis to the car, the front of his shirt was dripping with blood, he needed help. He moaned and not because of the pain.

“Don’t smack my car, Rob,” he said, wincing.

Now the adrenalin was wearing off, I could see the pain in his face and I gunned the car as fast as I could. We headed straight to the gym. Ted had a little flat above it and I banged on his door with one hand, the other around Travis's waist holding him up. A light came on and Ted, in shorts and a vest, opened his door. I knew then we looked worse than we felt by the utter shock on Ted's face. He rushed us straight in and I lay Travis down on the sofa.

Ted got towels and I pulled Travis's shirt free from his body. Slashes, some deep, some not so, crisscrossed over his chest, his stomach and there were many of them. He would be left with the scars from that night forever. Had I known just how much he had been hurt I would not have let that fat fucker live. Ted got on the phone straight away. I poured a whiskey and held up Travis's head so he could sip some. He hated whiskey, but it was the best pain killer Ted had in the flat.

"Rob, I'm going downstairs, there's a first aid kit somewhere in the gym," he said as he scuttled off. "I've rung Joe," he called out.

It took a few minutes for Ted to return with his first aid box and he unwrapped some gauze. He tried to stem the flow of blood from some of the deeper cuts but every time Travis winced and moved, another would open up again. Joe arrived, I heard him run up the stairs, behind him Mack and Paul who had bought Rosa, his wife. She pushed me to one side removing the gauze and inspected the cuts, she had brought a medical box with her.

"He needs to be in the hospital," she said in her soft Irish accent.

"No way lady," Travis said, wincing with the effort of speaking.

"Can you sort him out, Rosa?" I asked. She had been a nurse once, she would know what to do.

"Rob, what the fuck happened?" Joe asked.

"Not now, let me make sure Travis is okay first," I said.

Rosa got to work. She cleaned him up as best she could and stitched together the wounds, the whiskey softening the pain for him. She bandaged him and just before he passed out, he looked at me.

"You saved my life bro," he said.

"Rob, he will need antibiotics, he could get an infection, he really needs to be in hospital," she said. "Now, let me have a look at you." She winced at what she saw. "You both need to be in the hospital."

I had pulled my shirt over my head and looked at my side. A jagged cut ran down it, not the full length but long enough. Once cleaned it didn't look so bad, but every time I moved my arm, it opened again. It would need stitching too. Ted handed me a large glass of whiskey which I refused. Whiskey was the only thing I remembered from my childhood and something I avoided.

"Get on with it, Rosa," I said and I kept my gaze focused on my friend while she got to work.

Years later Mack would tell me that they had never seen anything like it. My eyes grew even darker and at no time did I flinch or wince as the needle weaved in and out, closing my wound.

"Mack, who the fuck did this? Who set my boys up? I want to know." Joe asked. I detected a very slight shake to his voice.

I knew who had done it but decided to keep quiet about that part for the moment. I told them where it had happened, someone would have to go and clean up. Whilst Joe headed back to the car I caught the attention of Mack.

"I know who it was and I want to deal with it myself," I growled. He nodded, I guess he had his suspicions himself.

Something changed in me then, I had killed two men. What little spark of hope I had for myself burnt out that day. I had been neglected, abused, left to live on a street to fight for a place to sleep, for food to eat and now I had killed again, and Joey had made that happen.

Chapter Three

Travis and I kept out of the way for a couple of weeks, we wanted to heal completely but we also wanted Joey to think we had run. Joe had put us up in one of his apartments in Columbia Heights. There was something that had been on my mind for years and I was in the mood for revenge. This was the perfect time, while we were out of town, to do something about avenging the first friend I ever had.

I had never told anyone about Cara or the fact that I blamed myself for her death. If I hadn't had freaked out that day, if I hadn't had fought the Father and brought the whole school out in the playground to stand and see Cara sobbing, her father might not have known. He might not have been called to the school to find out Cara had told me. It would have stayed our secret and she might have lived.

"Trav, there's something I need to do and I don't want to involve you in this," I told him one morning.

"Bro, everything you do involves me," he replied.

I told him everything, every sordid little detail of mine and Cara's life. Of how I had plans to run away, to save her from the misery she was going through. In one way it felt good to share something that had scarred me but in another I felt I was betraying Cara. I had promised to never tell and I hoped I would never have had to break that promise.

Without any hesitation Travis said, "Let's get going, Rob. Let's pay these men a visit."

We drove the few hours it took back to Pittsburgh and as I passed the wooden sign announcing we had arrived in the wonderful and friendly town of Sterling, my stomach turned with loathing. Nothing had changed. We pulled alongside a piece of barren land, the land where the house I had spent my childhood in had once stood. We parked the car and got out. Travis was silent as we walked to the edge of the trees. I knew every inch of those woods and he followed as I made my way through. It was still there, although not completely upright anymore, my camp, my hideaway, my sanctuary. I ran my fingers over Cara's and my initials, carved into the bark of a tree.

"I used to beg her to run away with me," I said quietly.

"Maybe she was just too scared," he said.

"Yeah, and I guess we wouldn't have got very far, not then."

First port of call was the church. I wanted to see if Father Peters was still around. The town was eerily quiet but as we passed the school, attached to the church, I could hear hymns being sung. A shiver went through me as I recalled being made to sit on the cold floor day after day and sing words of praise to a God I hated. I pushed through the unlocked doors of the church and walked to the front, to the pew I was made to sit every weekend. I paused looking at it, remembering the times I would get a slap to the back of my head because I wasn't praying hard enough. I remembered the times I would glance over to Cara, sitting opposite and we would share a smile. The church was empty yet, in my head, I heard the voices of my aunt, of the Father preaching his fire and brimstone sermons.

We made our way around the back of the church to the small cottage attached which, I hoped, Father Peters still lived in. There was no sign of anyone at the house and we walked around the side until we came to the small garden at the rear. A figure was hunched over using two canes to shuffle up the garden path. He halted before slowly turning around to face me. I looked at the broken body that was once the Father, the blue eye that was once brown.

"I've been expecting you, Robert," he whispered. "For years, I've been expecting you."

I stood, silently, and watched him. He had paid for his sins, by whose hand I wasn't sure although I had my suspicions. He reached out to me with his gnarled hand, I turned and walked away.

"I'm sorry. God forgive me, I'm sorry," he whispered to my retreating back.

I stopped and half turned. "You carrying on asking, Father, he isn't listening. He never did to those who needed him and he sure as fuck isn't going to listen to you."

The next stop was a run-down shack of a house on a small holding just a few miles away. The noise of the car had a woman come out through the broken screen door. She looked old, worn out, worn down by the life she had led, she held the hand of a small child although I doubted this was her own. She pulled the grubby child to her and cradled his face in her apron. I caught the sight of a chicken coop, two scrawny, uncared for chickens were scratching in the dirt. Neither of us spoke but she closed her eyes and nodded before pointing to a shed.

Quietly entering the shed, Travis and I made our way over to the old man fixing the rota blades of his tractor. He'd heard us and as he stood and turned, I punched him to the floor.

"What the...," was all he managed to say before he recognised me and his eyes widened in fear.

I crouched down in front of him. "Payback time, for Cara. Remember her? The daughter you abused, the daughter you killed," I snarled.

He started to snivel, his body shaking in fear as I paced, the hatred and disgust for this man pouring from me. For the first time I was struggling to gain control of myself. Every memory of that time flooded my brain, I found it hard to focus, to concentrate.

"You see, there isn't a day that goes by where I don't see her face, where I don't hear her cries. Do you? Does she haunt you like she does me? Do you close your eyes at night and see her face, the split lip, the bruises? Do you see the blood running down her thighs? I do and I never forgot."

Travis placed his hand on my shoulder, I stopped and looked at him. Without saying a word he gave a slight nod to his head and indicated with his eyes for me to move to one side. He then grabbed the man by his hair dragging him towards the still spinning rota blades, tipping him forwards so he instinctively put out his hands to stop his fall.

"You won't be laying your filthy hands on anyone, ever again now, will you?" Travis said.

As we walked out of the shed the woman, minus the child, stood outside.

"Thank you, Robert," she said as a tear rolled down her cheek. She turned and walked back to her house, ignoring the screams from her husband.

Did I feel good? No. There was nothing good about what Travis and I had done, but that man had abused every one of his children, his wife and God knows how many others. He had killed his daughter, a beautiful girl with blonde hair and kind, hazel eyes. He had never received punishment, the town never acknowledged what he had done. Was I judge and jury? In this case, yes, and justice had been served. He would live, but he would never be able to touch another person again.

As we headed back to the car, Travis pulled a wash cloth from the makeshift clothes line and wiped the blood splatters from his face. He gave me a smile as we climbed in the car and headed back to Washington. I rested my head back, closed my eyes and slept the whole way.

****

One evening, a few days later, Travis and I followed Joey to a bar. We watched him lord it up, play the hard man. The thing with Joey was that he had a big mouth, he wanted everyone to know who he was. He played on people knowing who his father was. He was the youngest of Joe's kids, short and stocky but not fit, with dank, greasy hair and a spotty face. He only got girls he paid for, and now he had made two very dangerous enemies in Travis and I.

We sat outside in the car, watching, waiting for him to leave. Stupidly he thought he was now untouchable, and to our surprise when he left the bar he walked. We waited until he had passed the car we sat in. I listened to his footsteps echoing along the now deserted street towards the house. Very quietly, Travis and I got out as he passed by and when we were close I watched his steps falter, he knew someone was behind him. He gave a slight look to his side, not wanting it to be obvious that he needed to check who was following him.

I reached out with one hand grabbing the back of his collar, pulling him towards me. I spun him around, I wanted him to know who was behind him and to see us. His face openly displayed the fear and the shock he was desperately trying to hide. I felt him tremble and then he opened his mouth.

"What the fuck do you think you are doing? Get your fucking hands of me," he said.

I dragged him back towards the open trunk of the car. Travis kicked at the back of his knees until he fell, face first, inside. We slammed the trunk shut and drove to the same warehouse Joey had selected for our demise. All the time he was shouting and bashing his fists against the trunk.

We pulled up alongside the warehouse and noticed there was a new padlock securing the door. Reaching behind the seat, Travis took a tyre iron to gain us access. Walking to the back of the car, I popped open the trunk. Joey was lying on his side, his eyes full of fear but he made no attempt to move. I reached in and grabbed the front of his shirt hauling him out. Pushing him through the door, I threw him to the floor. Travis's foot connected with his ribs, making a sickening crack that echoed around the dark room.

Travis laughed. "You prick, you think you can set us up?" He was more scary when he was laughing, he enjoyed hurting people.

"What are you idiots talking about?" Joey stammered between coughs and wheezes, his eyes darting from the one laughing and the one chillingly silent.

"You hurt me, Rob, and dad will crush you," he said.

I raised my eyebrows and allowed a small smirk to cross my face. I crouched down on my heels beside him.

"What do you think will happen when Joe finds out what you did? What will happen when he finds out you paid people to kill us? One of them still lives, Joey, only one, but what do you think will happen if he talks? You got three men killed that night."

Looking at the shock registering on his face, I continued.

"No, you hadn't thought that far ahead had you, you fucking idiot. Are you that fucking dumb? Do you think you could threaten us, set us up, try to get us killed and then just walk away? And what's more insulting, is that you thought all we were worth was a kilo of coke."

With that I pulled back my fist and smashed it straight into his face, blood spurted from his nose. His hands covered his face and his bladder gave way. While piss soaked the front of his pants, Travis kicked him continuously. Joey curled up in a ball, crying for his mother. I took out the knife I carried and I held it to his face, his eyes widened as I sliced across his forehead and through his eyebrow.

"Every time you touch that scar, every time you see it, you'll be reminded of this night," I said.

"If you even so much as breathe the same air as us, Joey, I will slit your throat. The only reason you will live tonight is because I have more respect for your father than you do," I continued.

We left him there, sobbing into the dusty ground, knowing he would be pissing blood for the next week or so, but he would never forget what went on there, and would be constantly looking over his shoulder.

****

I needed sex. Whenever I fought, whenever my adrenalin was pumped, that was what I needed as a release. We headed to the club, it was nearly closing time but I knew the usual girls would be there. I had started to have regular sex with Christy. We would meet up two or three times a week and had been for about a year. I didn't view her as my girlfriend and whether she realised it, she was not the only girl I fucked. She was okay looking, blonde, wore too much make up and regularly hinted at having a conventional relationship. I liked the arrangement, she shared an apartment with another girl, worked in an office and was a couple of years older than me.

Walking into the club, there she was. I strode over, grabbed her by the arm and we made our way out. Travis gestured to Carly and the four of us headed out to their apartment, stopping at the liquor store to buy a six pack on the way.

Leaving Travis and Carly, we walked into Christy's bedroom. I still had Joey's blood on my fist and I was pumped. She undressed herself, knowing what I wanted and walked towards me, placing her arms around my neck and lifted her face to mine. I pulled her arms away, I didn't want intimacy with her, with anyone, I just wanted to fuck her.

I turned her to face the bed. I pushed at the base of her neck until she was bent over, supporting herself by her arms on the side of the bed. With my foot I kicked her legs apart and ran my hand over her ass, sliding it down and between her thighs, finding her clitoris already soaking wet. As I stroked and teased, I unzipped my pants. She moaned, pushing her body back towards me. I wrapped one hand in her hair, holding her head up and I slammed into her. I fucked her hard. I saw her legs shake as her orgasm built and she came. My release was quick to follow. But I wasn't finished.

As I kicked off my shoes, I pulled my shirt over my head. Christy gripped the side of my pants and slid them down. Before they had even fallen to the floor she had my cock in her mouth. My hands tangled in her hair and I fucked her mouth. I heard her gag, I saw tears form in her eyes and as they fell, a line of black mascara ran down her cheek.

I felt like a complete shit because I couldn't feel anything for her. I didn't love her, I was completely selfish in what I was doing. The least I could do was make sure she had a good time. She was on her knees, on the bed and as I climbed on, she lay down on her back beside me. My hand grazed over her nipple, twisting and squeezing and her body arched upwards. I let my hand slide down her stomach and she parted her legs. She was wet, a mixture of her and my come. I pushed two fingers in her, my thumb circled her clitoris and I watched her hands grip the bedding. As she came again, a flash of sadness washed over me. It took me by surprise and I wasn't entirely sure why.

I could hear the laughter from the other bedroom and it struck me that, Christy and I fucked, we didn't have fun doing it. There was never laughter from us.

She rolled onto me, riding my cock while her hands splayed on my chest. She bent down to kiss me but I turned my face slightly away, her lips only connecting with the side of my mouth. I held her hips, mine rising and falling to meet her rhythm and as her head fell back and she cried out my name, I came.

“Will you stay the night?” she asked after, a pleading in her voice. I didn’t answer.

I was sat on the end of her bed. She’d pulled the sheet around herself, covering her naked body and I heard a small sob. I wasn’t capable of a relationship with anyone, I thought she had understood that. I knew I used her for my own satisfaction, I knew she would have loved to have a proper relationship with me, but this was all I could offer. She could do a whole lot better than lust after me. I turned, ran my fingers down her cheek, my thumb rubbing away at some of the black under one eye and I looked at her.

“Chris, I don’t want a relationship, with anyone. I’m sorry if you think I’m using you and I guess I am really, but this is all you will get from me. I can’t give you any more,” I said gently. I stood and dressed.

Back then I knew I didn’t treat women fairly, I took what I wanted, giving them nothing back. I didn’t love her, I liked her enough to want to have sex with her but I found it hard to respect her, she just gave in, accepting whatever little I would offer her. I had nothing in me to give to another person, other than Travis. We were bound together for life after what we had been through. I walked away leaving her crying, calling for Travis who sounded like he was having a better time than I’d had and we left.

I didn’t have sex because I wanted that connection with a woman, it was more of a release for me, emotionless fucking. Travis fell in love with every girl, albeit there would be a new one each week.

****

The following night we got pulled by the cops. As we left the club, I noticed a car pull out behind us, its blue lights flashing.

“What do you want to do bro?” Travis asked.

“Pull over, let’s see what they want.”

Travis pulled over to the curb and we waited for the occupants of the car behind to arrive. A cop tapped at the driver window.

“Permit,” he said.

Travis rifled around the car until he found what they wanted.

“Exit the car, slowly, both of you,” we were instructed.

Two police officers, who had obviously been waiting, gestured for us to get out. We were made to face the car as they handcuffed us and took us to the station.

“Do you want to tell me what this is about?” I asked while we were sitting in the back of their car.

“We’re investigating an assault, thought you might like to help us with that,” I was told.

“And you need to handcuff me to do that?”

As much as we had never been pulled up by the cops before, I knew being handcuffed and forced into the back of their car, driven to the station, was not normal.

Standing at the counter, we were asked our names, our pockets were searched, keys and money was placed in a tray. I had thrown the knife after I had used it on Joey and I now thanked my instinct for that, perhaps I had known this might happen.

We were placed in separate cells, the smallness of them was something that I hated. There were no windows, a single bulb hung from the ceiling, its flickering light only just casting a glow over the room. Its incessant hum would drive me mad if I’d had to stay in that cell too long. There was a metal cot along one wall and a stainless steel toilet against another. I stood, I wouldn’t sit on the cot, the mattress was stained and dirty.

Eventually the door opened, a plain clothed cop asked me to follow him. We entered a small room with just a table, a couple of chairs and a tape recorder which was switched on, waiting to record every word that was spoken. I was offered coffee, a cigarette, both of which I declined, so far the cop had been pleasant.

“Robert, my name is Detective Jones and this here is Detective Mallory,” he introduced the one standing by the door.

I wondered which one was going to play the bad cop and Mallory seemed to fit the bill. He had puffed out his chest and crossed his arms, resting them on the gut that overflowed the top of his trousers.

"I have a couple of questions you might be able to help me answer," he said.

He already knew my name, knew who I was. "First, I don't appreciate being handcuffed and left in a cell just to help you with your enquiries. However, saying that, what would you like my help with?" I asked.

I wanted to make sure the fact that we had been handcuffed and left in a cell was recorded.

"Joey Morietti," he said. "Wound up in the hospital, someone has done him over good, know anything about that?"

"No, I don't," I replied.

"So, anyone you can think of who would?"

"No."

"Did he have enemies?"

"I guess you need to ask him that."

"I would imagine, in your line of business, there would be plenty of people waiting for a little payback," he said.

"I don't know what line of business Joey is in," I replied.

It was obvious this guy was not going to get too much out of me and Mallory walked from his position, holding up the wall.

"We know that you know him. We know you work for his father," he said.

"I haven't denied knowing him. I have explained that I was not aware he had been done over, as you put it, or who would have done that," I replied.

"Are you not concerned for your friend?" he asked.

"He's not my friend and, if he has been done over, perhaps he has offended someone. But that someone was not me. I don't have anything to do with him. My business is with his father, as you rightly pointed out."

"So, what exactly do you do for his father?"

"Am I here answering questions about Joey, or his father?"

“You’re here answering whatever questions I want you to,” he replied.

“You have a reputation, Robert, we know you’re capable of doing this,” Jones said.

“Then if you have any evidence to that fact, perhaps you should charge me. Before you do, I have the right to call a lawyer.”

“Why would you need a lawyer? Right now you’re just helping with our enquiries,” he said.

“Has Joey made a complaint? Has he indicated I was the one to put him in the hospital?”

The look on their faces told me the answer was no. At least Joey had picked up one thing from his upbringing, omerta, the code of silence. I was surprised he hadn’t told the cops who had done him over though.

“Then, I have been kept here for over two hours. I’m tired and hungry so unless you want to charge me with something, it’s time for me to say goodnight,” I said as I stood.

I towered over both of them, my face showing no emotion.

“We still have a couple of questions,” Mallory said, blocking my route.

“About Joey or his father?” I asked.

“I’ll ask you again, what do you do for Guiseppi?”

“I collect his rents as I am sure you already know.”

“What do you do, Robert, when someone doesn’t pay? Beat up on little old women do you?”

Mallory was trying to rile me. I smiled, a cold chilling smile.

“Do I look like I need to beat up on little old women?” I asked.

They had no answer to that and with Mallory stepping to one side, I made for the door.

“You can let Mr. Morietti know that we will be doing everything we can to catch the people who put his son in hospital,” he said, a veiled threat.

“I’m sure, as a tax payer, he’ll be pleased to hear that. Now, I expect Travis will be ready to leave as well.”

While I waited for Travis, I collected my money and keys and headed outside.

"Hey bro, you okay?" I heard as he came out of the station.

"Sure, let's get a cab back to the car," I replied.

We didn't talk about it until we were back to where we had left the car and the first thing we did was to make sure the tail lights were not all of a sudden broken, another reason we could be pulled over.

"What did they ask you?" I said

"About Joey, wanted to know who had done him over. I told them we were at the club, guess they checked but other than that not much else."

"They wanted to know what we did for Joe, I said we collected rent," I told him.

He nodded. "Think this might be a regular thing?"

"Probably, now I'm starving, let's go find something to eat," I said as we headed off.

It was a couple of days later that Mack pulled me to one side.

"Joey is in the hospital, you know anything about that?" he asked.

I told him what had happened, how the lorry had not arrived and the envelope that should have been full of money was full of cocaine, how I'd hid it but carried on to the warehouse. I told him about the four men, what I had done to two of them, what they had done to Travis and how I had let one go because, to live a life of fear was worse than dying. He would have known some of this, he would have been the one to organise a clean up. I also told him about the tug from the cops. The fact that the cops had let us leave without too much trouble was something to think about. They could have kept us there for longer, they could have trumped up some charges that would later get dropped but would inconvenience us, something didn't add up.

He nodded, "Joe needs to know, Rob."

"Not yet, Mack. Wait a bit, let's see what Joey does next, but tell him about the cops. They were asking about his activities," I replied.

Joe was still occupied for the next couple of weeks with Joey, leaving me and Travis with the guys. We moved around the business as we had before but this time I wanted a say and to my surprise, it was welcomed.

"Jon, don't you want this all legit? We could make a lot more money if it was," I asked Jonathan one day.

"Well, Joe is getting older, he has talked about taking a bit of a back seat for a while. To be honest it might be good to not have to keep looking over our shoulder all the time."

What had happened to Travis and I had unnerved them. They had all seen their fair share of violence, especially Mack, over the years but now they had families, children and it was time to settle down. A plan was hatched. I would study each business and present to Joe how it could be made legal, better, more profitable and how he could filter his money into legitimate business.

****

A little over a month later Joey made his first visit to the office, he took a seat outside while I was sitting with Joe and the guys going through plans, first the construction side. This was easy, Joe already had a building company, all it meant was for all monies to go through the books, every purchase to be accounted for and proper building applications submitted. I explained how much easier it would make life. With Jonathan's help, we explained about the tax benefits. The properties Joe already owned were okay, what they needed was proper supervision. If we got the repairs done and redecorate, we could attract a better tenant and higher rents.

The loan business could be licensed but it caused more hassle than was worth it really, I suggested that we let it go. The cigarettes and booze, well, that was just plain hijacking and there was not much that could be made legal about that.

The drugs were another thing I wanted out of. I knew that Joey was dealing, cocaine and heroin, I also knew that Joe would not be happy about that. If the police were starting to nose around, they could mistake this for his activities. Now was the time to cut Joey loose.

"Joe, you know that night?" I said, I didn't have to say more, he knew exactly what I was talking about

"Yeah, Mack is still looking into that," he replied.

"Well, there's no need. I know who set us up and I've dealt with him. He'll walk around with a permanent reminder not to fuck with me," I said, referring to the scar left on Joey's face.

He looked at me, his features hard and I could see a pulse pounding in his temple. The room stilled as his face showed that he had understood what I was saying.

"That prick Joey did it, didn't he? That fucker set you up and for what? Have I not treated him well, not treated you all the same? He does that to his brother?" he shouted.

It was obvious the pain he was in, his own flesh and blood had arranged for his adopted sons to be hurt, to be killed.

"Joey, get the fuck in here," he shouted.

A very timid Joey entered the office, his eyes darting from me to his father. Joe jumped up from behind his desk and paced to where Joey stood, his face puce with anger. Joe seemed to struggle for breath and sweat beaded on his forehead. I stood, walked over and placed my hand on his shoulder, he was getting too old for all this shit. His heart was not good and as much as he needed to know what Joey had done, I didn't want him to be that stressed.

He looked up at me. I towered over him and for the first time I really saw him, a tired old man albeit only in his sixties. He'd had a hard life and it showed, now it was time for him to sit back a little, enjoy the rest of his life. There were many people out on the streets wanting a piece of his action, a lot younger and willing to shoot for it. The world was changing, the old school attitude would not keep Joe from losing what he had, there was little respect anymore.

"Joey, what you did was wrong and for what, jealousy? You can't be trusted. You skim money off every collection you make, you're stealing from your own father. And did you know that crack you sold to Macy's kid, he died, Joey," I said standing side by side with Joe.

The room quietened, the guys watched and Joe stared at me. Macy was a woman who lived nearby, she regularly asked to borrow a bit of money, to tie her over until her next pay check. She was a decent woman trapped in a shit life with a drug addict for a son. A now dead son. Joe wasn't aware of what had happened, it was something we had kept from him until we were sure Joey was his dealer.

"This is what's going to happen, Joey. You're going to leave, you're no good to us. You want the drugs, you take it but you will not peddle your shit on our streets. You get on with your life doing whatever the fuck you want but if you so much as breathe a word about what you know, what has gone on here, I will fucking bury you," I told him, my voice quiet and menacing.

"Do you agree with this?" Joey shouted at his father. "Are you going to stand by and let him do this, take what should be mine? Listen to him "our streets". Since when has he been in charge, huh?"

He turned to look at Jonathan. "You're the Consigliere, do your fucking job and advise dad. This is bullshit."

"I work for your father, Joey, not you. And Joe, Rob is right, you need to cut him loose," Jonathan replied.

Joey was starting to panic, it was clear he would never receive the support nor the respect he thought he had.

"We can earn money, dad, lots of it, people want the drugs. You get them addicted, they have to come back for more. You're letting him take this away from us and if you do that, you're a spineless prick."

I took a step closer, I would not tolerate him disrespecting his father that way. He had the life he had because of him. He never had to really work. He had a new car every year, new clothes, money in his pocket because of what his father did. More importantly, he had neither the brains nor the capacity to take over. Joe and every person in that room, that day, knew it.

"Dad, you don't want this, you guys don't want him running the family, do you?" Joey asked, looking around the room.

No one answered him.

"Joey, my son. You are my flesh and blood and I love you but, as Robert has said, you are a liability. I know what you do and it pains me, here," Joe said, pointing to his heart.

"It pains me, Joey, that you think I am fucking stupid, blind and without ears. That shit you sell kills, Joey, it kills." Joe was shouting.

"And you haven't," Joey shouted back.

"I haven't what?" Joe replied, confused.

"You're not a saint, dad, you brought me up in this fucking life, you've killed, I know you have."

"I have never killed anyone, and I did wrong. I should have kept you out, like your sisters," Joe replied, a sadness creeping into his voice.

"Oh, Saint Evelyn and the nutter, Maria. Yeah, you did good dad, real good. And what about my mother, huh? Did you make her life so shit that it killed her?" Joey spat the words.

"Don't you dare mention your mother, the cancer killed her," Joe shouted.

Joe took a step closer, his body shaking, I guessed with anger. I placed my arm across his shoulder, halting his advance and closed the gap myself.

"You are dangerously close to seeing just how angry I can get. Your father loved your mother, she died from an illness," I said.

"What the fuck would you know, huh? You think you are his son, you're nothing but a fucking street kid. You should be kissing his feet he took you and that prick in."

From the corner of my eye I watched Travis move so fast, closing the gap between him and Joey. Thankfully Mack was there to block his way.

"Not here, not now," Mack said.

"If you want to take me on, take Travis on, you are heading the right way. As you already know, that's something you need to think real hard about," I said.

He pointed, jabbing his finger at me. "You won't get away with this," he shouted, without a huge amount of conviction.

"I just did. Remember what I said that night, Joey. Now fuck off out of my sight before I change my mind and bury you now," I said, my eyes dead of any emotion.

He turned and walked away, slamming the door so hard, the windows rattled in their frames. The only sound was a release of breath from Joe who seemed to have aged yet another ten years in that moment. I led him by the arm back to his desk, gestured with my hand for him to take his seat so we could carry on before we were interrupted. He stopped mid way, looking at that chair he had sat in, at that desk, for the past forty years. He stared up at me, his eyes full of unshed tears and shook his head, a sad smile crossed his lips.

"Rob, you sit, you have the respect of everyone here, me included. I trust you to deal with this, I think it's time for me to take a back seat. I'm tired," he said sadly and he walked out of that office, sealing my fate.

I looked from one guy to the next, I wanted confirmation that they were with me on this. They too were getting on, in their forties, they had all led a life of looking over their shoulders and most had families to protect. I wanted for us all to have a better future, a more secure, safer one.

Each in turn nodded their agreement, Paul a little more hesitantly than the others, but he was good at what he did, I didn't want to have to go into battle with him. I had learnt enough over the past couple of years to understand exactly what each did, their strengths and weaknesses and I wanted them to be part of what I thought was the future for us all.

"So, here's what we're going to do," I said, taking my place at the desk.

To celebrate, Travis and I took ourselves off to a tattoo parlour. I knew exactly what I wanted, something I had drawn a long time ago, something that was significant to me and especially at that time of my life.

An angel, not just any angel but a fallen one. An angel rejected by God because she had chosen to sin. I had spent from the age of eleven choosing to sin. I always knew exactly what I was doing and for a long time I enjoyed it. Only now did I want a different way of life.

Chapter Four

It took a couple of years to really lose the crap and turn around the rest. We formed various companies, we paid as little tax as we could legally get away with and we made money, lots of it. Once a week I sat down with Joe and told him what we were doing, it was important to me that he was in the loop. In the meantime, he enjoyed his semi retirement. Evelyn was grateful to us, we had finally got the old man to relax a little, to potter around his garden and enjoy his wealth.

It didn't come without problems. We had a couple of new gangs on the street trying to muscle in before we were ready. Travis and I still got into the occasional fight, settling some dispute or other, showing who was still in charge.

We spent the first year updating the apartments, redecorating and with a little coercion, removed the low rent tenants and replaced them with better ones. The only one I was a little sad to see go was old Mrs Wren and her cats. We made sure we found somewhere for her to live. Not too far from the apartments was a low rise block where the residents were mainly elderly and were able to keep an eye out on her. She had a small back yard, somewhere for her cats to roam.

We saw nothing of Joey but we kept track of him for a while. He had decided selling drugs was going to make his fortune, but he was one man, no back up against some serious competition. I was often approached by one dealer or another and kept informed of what he was doing. They did this because I was still someone to be respected. I allowed them on my streets to sell their shit. It went against what I believed, but I could control who and what went on. People would always want drugs, we were in a low income environment and no matter whether their kids went hungry, the people living there still had money for drugs.

We had not lost everything we did, there was still the odd personal debt to collect but I wasn't involved on a street level anymore. I had grown up a lot in the past couple of years. A powerful man I was always told, although still only early twenties. At twenty-two I earned my first million dollars with many more to follow over the next ten years. That first million was a huge milestone in my life. I was no longer hungry, no longer poor, I wore the best clothes, owned the best cars and now I wanted somewhere to live. It was time to move out of Joe's, to leave the comfort of the only real home I'd ever known.

****

Although we kept the small office, a reminder of where we started, a development opportunity come up and we moved. It was to be a purpose built complex in the heart of DC and I had the top floor converted to an apartment, three bedrooms where Travis and I would live. Evelyn came and looked after the place for us. To start, we rented out most of the floors in the office block but as each section of the company grew we took them back, for staff. We decided that we would start an umbrella company, bring everything under one roof. Vassago Corporation was formed and Joe finally retired completely. He handed over most of the companies to me. The ones I didn't want, I let go and others I paid a small price for. Joe understood that the money he had accumulated over the past few years was because of the work I had put in, and as much as I earned very well, he only wanted a small price.

"Why Vassago?" Joe asked me one day.

We were sitting side by side in his summer room drinking espresso. I smiled, it was my little secret but I would share it with him.

"Vassago was a fallen angel, Joe, but one with a good heart. He's the discoverer of the lost and hidden," I said.

For the first time ever, he pulled me in to a hug.

"Rob, you have lived the life you've had to. You have done well and there are many people indebted to you. You have made their lives rich and I don't mean just with money. You are a good person, it's time to believe that. Vassago," he said with a laugh. "I like it. You, Rob, are the discoverer of the lost and hidden."

It took me many years to fully understand what he meant.

Vassago owned stores it rented out, a hotel, a couple of bars, a restaurant, five tenant blocks, a construction company and a realtor. Property worth millions. Managing this was easy. I placed each of the guys in charge of one section and gave them shares in Vassago as a thank you for their loyalty to Joe and I.

Each division had one or two floors, depending on the level of staff. Paul heading construction, Richard had properties, Jonathan headed his team of admin, accountants and marketing. Mack and Travis dealt with security, we were still aware of our enemies, some from the past and no doubt we would acquire some new, legitimate ones.

The first real argument I had with Travis was over the business. I wanted him to have a share, to be part of it, but he was and still is a street kid at heart. He knew he would be no good sitting in an office all day but what he was good at was his quick thinking, his ability to detect trouble and he was the ultimate gadget man. There wasn't a computer around he couldn't hack into. I left him with Mack, they worked well as a team but I always had him by my side, he was the one who had always driven and this continued. We were brothers, inseparable by a bond that had formed many years ago.

"Trav, I want you to be part of this company," I had told him.

"Rob, I don't want it. Listen, I still have family, one sniff of a bit of money and who knows what will crawl out of the woodwork. I earn well, you've looked after me and what the fuck do I know about running a business."

"That's not the point. No one can take away what you earn, whoever they are. You deserve this. You've been here the whole time, you've got your hands dirty over the years, now it's time to share in it."

"No, you know me. I'd be bored shitless I gotta start working for a living," he laughed.

The problem with Travis was that he'd had no education really. Sure he could read and write, but he was more a man of action. No matter what, I would make sure he got his share whether he wanted it or not. I set up a bank account in his name and he would earn well, whatever profit share I was entitled to, I split with him. I had enough money to last me my lifetime.

****

One of the other events that had a great affect on my life was Evelyn. She had been dating Carlo for a while, someone Joe liked. I had met the guy quite a few times, there was something about him I didn't like but I would not voice my opinion. She had cared for her father, Joey and her sister, Maria, who had been sick for so many years now. She cared for Travis and I, and now it was time for her to think about herself.

She still fussed over us, still fed us and spent her whole time trying to create as normal a life for us as was possible. She was oblivious to a lot that went on and I wanted it that way. I loved, in my own way, three people only, Travis, her and Joe. They were the only people I was able to have a connection with, the only people able to affect me. So when Carlo proposed, I was pleased for her. I knew, however, that he didn't like how she was with Travis and I. It was not jealousy, we were her brothers, but he didn't like the connection the three of us had, the bond we shared that he could not be part of, could not break. He understood, but didn't like that he would always share her with us. He hated that we had developed this silent communication between us, an understanding of each other he would never get.

But he had me all wrong. If he took her away from us, I would be pleased. She had this compulsion to look after us and it would always affect any relationship she had. I wanted better for her, to be able to leave us. We would never lose contact but for her to be a wife, a mother, to have a normal life was all I ever wanted for her. There was no chance of that for Travis and I, so if one of us could, then great.

On the day he proposed, Carlo came to see me to talk about the wedding. I found this disrespectful to Joe and told him so. That conversation should have been with the father of the bride, not me. It also showed how uneasy he was about me. It was my first insight into how far I had come but how I was still viewed as the head of this family, which was something I didn't want.

I'd met with Joe that night, our weekly meetings still continued although he had no official say, but I valued his opinion and I treasured the relationship we had. I didn't tell him Carlo had come to me, I wouldn't hurt him that way. To an Italian, to know his daughter's prospective husband had overlooked him would be a huge insult. We chatted late into the night. It was good to be able to spend that time with him, he had been so important in my life, but he was getting old and poorly. I was also grateful that over the years I had learnt his language. As he got older he became increasingly Italian, reverted to his native tongue more often than speaking in English.

Evelyn joined us, she told her father about the proposal and like me, he was pleased for her. To see her face light up as she spoke about Carlo saddened me, not that it showed. I didn't believe I would ever feel that way about someone, I simply didn't have the ability to. We talked about wedding plans, she wanted Travis and I involved as much as possible but I drew the line at her having brides-men.

A day or so after Evelyn had agreed to marry Carlo though, I started to see the stress in her face. I would often ask her if everything was okay but she would lie and tell me all was fine. I had to bide my time, she would tell me what was bothering her when she wanted to. It became known a couple of weeks later. She had come to visit me at work, something she did regularly and brought me lunch to make sure I ate.

"Hi, are you busy?" she said, popping her head around the door.

I would always have time for her, she knew that. She sat, opened her bag, she had made sandwiches for us and while she ate, she said, "I've broken it off with Carlo, I thought I would tell you first."

"Why, Ev? I thought you loved him?" I said.

"I don't think I ever really did, Robert, and I love you and Travis more," she said sadly.

"But you'll still see us," I replied, confused.

"He wants me to choose, you boys or him and I can't do that," she said quietly.

"What the fuck does he mean, choose between us?" I replied, anger building up in me.

“Rob, please, don’t get angry. No matter what man I meet, they have to share me with you. It’s my choice and he isn’t strong enough to do that.”

I looked at her and my heart broke. There was such a bond between us, it would take a special person to accept that, I understood, but it made me feel guilty.

“Please don’t be sad for me, Rob, I’m not. It’s the right thing to do. I want to spend my life with you guys and if he’s not the right person to accept that, then to marry him would be wrong,” she told me.

I went to see Carlo later that day, he worked with his father, selling cars. I’d thought him a little sleazy and this was proven right when I watched him slouched over the desk of the receptionist, she was giggling and tossing her hair at him. He was loving it. He and Evelyn had only broken up that day, he could have least shown some sadness. I strode across the room, catching his eye immediately.

“Carlo, I would like to have a word,” I said, carrying on past him to a vacant office.

“What can I do for you, Robert?” he asked, closing the door behind us.

“I would like to know what went on with you and Evelyn. She told me something I found a little disturbing earlier today.”

“What can I say, she broke it off,” he said with a shrug of his shoulders. However, he did look a little uncomfortable.

“And why was that Carlo? What caused her to change her mind?” I asked.

“Erm, well, perhaps you should ask her,” he stammered.

“I have. She told me that you asked her to choose, you or us. I take it you don’t love her enough to accept she has family?” I stated.

He had the grace to look away.

“Clearly you don’t, so why propose in the first place?” I asked.

“Look, Rob, we’re both guys right. She’s a great girl and all that, she would have made a great wife but I wanted her to talk to you, she wouldn’t. I could be a great asset to you.”

This threw me somewhat.

"My name is Robert, only those close to me can call me Rob," I said, understanding now what had gone on.

"So, let me get this straight. You dated Evelyn because you thought it was your way in to the family and our business. When she refused to speak to me, your retaliation was to ask her to choose between you and us. You used her."

He didn't need to answer, and as I walked slowly towards him, he shuffled from foot to foot.

"If I hear that you have been in contact with her, even a nod across the street, I'll come for you," I said.

He looked down at his shuffling feet.

"Do you understand what I just said?" I asked.

He nodded.

What hurt the most was the realisation that the people around me could get used and hurt as a way to get to me. Whether it be, like Carlo, they simply wanted to work for me, or maybe because they wanted to get to me. I would have to be careful, I would have to protect those closest to me so that could never happen again. I arranged a security team, everyone we met with would be vetted, to see what their motives were. Maybe it was overkill but Travis and I had enemies, the whole team did, but I had not banked on Evelyn being used.

I was devastated for her, although she had called off the farce of a wedding, I thought she had been in love with him, she thought he had loved her too. That was always going to be a problem and something I would have to think hard about. Perhaps the answer was to push Evelyn away a little, break the connection so that she was free to go, to choose a man over us. The thought that she was so tied to me and Travis that she did not have the freedom she deserved, upset me greatly.

"Trav, we need to talk," I said as I got back in the car.

I told him what had happened, what Carlo's real intentions were and I confessed to being upset about it. He turned in his seat to face me.

“Rob, look at you, look at what you’ve become, what you’ve achieved. People are in awe of you and sadly neither of us will ever be able to shake off the lifestyle we’ve led. There are always going to be people that want to get close to you and they’ll use whatever, whoever they can, to do that,” he said.

“It’s wrong, Trav. Why should Ev not have a life beyond us? It’s not fair on her,” I replied.

“Bro, if anything, you’ll have more enemies now than before. By becoming legit, we’re all vulnerable, there will always be someone from the past who has enough knowledge to damage us,” he said.

“Mmm, maybe we need to step up security a bit.”

What I didn’t say was that I felt there was no hope for me, probably not for Travis either, to have a normal life, a normal relationship, get married, have kids. I could have lived that through Evelyn, watched her have the life I wanted and enjoy it that way.

Instead, every person we got close to, Evelyn got close to, I would now always question their motives. I found it hard to trust people at the best of times and that just made it worse.

****

The businesses were doing well. We had spent a great deal of money on renovating the apartment blocks, especially the ones in Columbia Heights. The state were installing a new subway, the whole area was having a makeover and it allowed us to attract better tenants, higher rentals. Construction was up, we had developments in New York starting soon and I would make the trip out there to meet with the teams as the projects progressed. Doing anything in New York was a little harder than Washington, I was to have a meeting with the Gioletti family. As much as I was not prepared to have involvement with any other crime family, they could cause me problems if I didn’t have them on side.

The Gioletti’s were an old family and connected to Joe, and I had no doubt they still had activities in crime, although much of what they did was legal. However, the development I was planning was in the middle of their territory, so to speak. So, to enable smooth progress, it was a matter of meet, show a little respect and hopefully we would have no problems.

Paul, Travis and I took the short flight and made our way to New York City. First I wanted to see the site, understand the neighbourhood, get a feel for who would be affected by what we were doing. At that time property was booming, development was in progress all over the state and we wanted a piece of the action. Travis was uncomfortable though, this had been his home town. I had talked to him about getting in contact with his family, his dad was long dead but his mother was still alive. He would have none of it, he was still bitter and he felt his mother had done nothing to try to stop what happened to him, his brothers and sister and I could relate to that.

We were met at the site by Massimo Gioletti and his guys. Although now well in his fifties, he was still an imposing man. He stood in silence for a moment or two, sizing me up. I stood my ground, I held his gaze and once that was over, he greeted me warmly.

“Massimo, thank you for taking the time to meet with me,” I said, offering him my respect.

“Robert, it’s good to finally meet you too. Now tell me, how is Guiseppi? My father and he were great friends, years ago back in Chicago,” he told me.

“He’s doing okay, his heart’s not so good and he has cancer, but he’s enjoying his retirement. He sends his regards to you and your family,” I replied.

The two of us walked around the site and I detailed what we wanted to do, how we would also be willing to spend a little on the neighbourhood. We would create a park area for the children of the families who would eventually live here. He nodded his approval.

“I wanted to meet with you Massimo, out of respect to you and your family, but not for your approval. I want to ensure that Vassago will be able to complete this development without any issues, without any disruption. I am not in the game of bribes, back handers or favours, that style has long past. I have an opportunity here and I want it completed,” I said gently.

He looked at me.

"You're a new breed, Robert, Guiseppi should be proud of you. I've heard a lot about you over the years. It's a shame I don't have anyone of your calibre here, in New York," he laughed.

"I hear your son, Luca, is doing well for you."

"Ah, Luca, he fills his head with the old days, perhaps watches too many movies," he replied with a laugh.

"Do you still fight?" he asked.

"Only for fun and generally with Travis," I replied.

"I watched one of your fights once, you were very angry if I remember," he said with a chuckle.

"Probably. I was angry a lot back then."

"And not now?" he enquired.

"Only when the need arises, Massimo."

"It's been good to follow your progress, Robert. You have done well for your family, for Guiseppi. I don't foresee any problems with your development. Perhaps, in the future, we may have a joint project," he said.

"Thank you, I have enjoyed our talk."

The comment about following my progress was his way of letting me know he had been keeping an eye on my business, especially in New York. I understood because, when we decided to build there, we had done the same. As for any future projects, well, that would depend.

I shook his hand, he pulled me into a hug, kissed both my cheeks and I left for home, deal done. He knew where I stood and I thanked him for his time. It was with a little sadness that I learnt a couple of years later that Massimo had been arrested, many charges placed against him for his earlier lifestyle and he would probably spend the rest of his days in prison.

****

"Hi, Joe, how are you today?" I asked as I arrived at his home. I wanted to let him know what had happened in Manhattan.

"Rob, come and sit with me," he wheezed.

I had noticed how frail he had become over the past couple of months and I worried for him. He had been to the doctors, had test after test until cancer had been diagnosed. He was now nearing his seventies and Evelyn still fussed over him every day.

"Massimo sends his regards, he told me you and his father went back a long way."

He chuckled. "That we did, Rob. Do you want me to tell you about it?"

All Joe had was his garden, his daughters and his memories. I liked to sit with him and listen to his life story and when he talked about Italy, I vowed I would visit his village one day and experience his culture.

"Carmine Gioletti and I were friends from the village, we were about the same age although he died some time ago. When I arrived in Chicago he was already there, a member of a gang called the Outfit and I worked with him. He was a good man, I learnt a lot from him and he and I stayed friends. Trouble was, I didn't want any part of the drugs and that was where they earned much of their money. I didn't like the way the family was heading and he understood that. Did you know my wife, Maria, was his first cousin?" he asked.

No, I hadn't. The two families were obviously more connected than I thought. It would have been because of that connection that Massimo returned the respect I had shown him.

"I met her back home, her family lived near mine. She was the most beautiful thing I had laid eyes on and I fell in love with her, instantly. I will tell you this, Robert. I fought hard to get her, she had a real independent streak, but I won in the end. I got the greatest prize, Maria and then three children. It's all a man should ever want, the love of a good woman," he said, his eyes glazing over with the memory.

"You will experience it one day, Rob, and it will change your life. To feel that depth of love from someone is a wonderful thing. Now, help me up, I've had enough talk of love, I want to walk and you can tell me about this building project."

We walked for a bit around his garden, I held his arm as he struggled, wincing in pain every now and again. He was a stubborn old fool, he had refused any treatment, not that it would cure him but it might have alleviated some of the pain he was clearly in.

"I told Massimo that I was not there for his permission, just assurance the project would not have any disruptions," I said.

Joe laughed, coughing at the same time. "I bet he was impressed with that."

"Funnily enough, he was okay with it. I don't want to be connected, Joe, we've moved on. All I want is for this project to get off the ground and make money."

"Rob, you put too much importance on making money," he said, waving my hand away as I tried to help him walk.

"With money, Joe, comes respect and that's all I want. For people to respect me."

"And they do, already. They also still fear you. I have ears, I still listen and you want to keep that, one day you might need it. You say you want no part of the old ways but, Robert, you're wrong. The old ways, the people still in that life will always be on the fringes of your new one, you will never break completely free," he warned me.

"It's not something that I want though," I replied.

He stopped walking, resting one hand on the back of a bench before turning to me.

"No matter where you were born, Robert, our way of life, it's in here," he said, his fingers tapping against my chest above my heart.

"I've no doubt you are at least part Italian, look at you. Even as a part bred, Robert, you live and breathe Italy, I brought you up to lover her. You don't escape her because you want to," he said.

I had learnt a long time ago that Joe believed Italy and the Cosa Nostra as one and the same, as did many of the older generation brought up in that life. It wasn't a lifestyle choice, for many it was, simply, the only way of life.

"You are my son, Robert, and I am proud of you, of what you are. Be proud as well," he said.

****

I got a call, around midnight, a week later from Evelyn, she was asking for me to come urgently. Joe had taken a turn for the worse over the previous couple of days. Travis and I sped through the night and arrived at his house. He was in his bed, propped up with pillows and now a very frail man. The three of us sat and I took his hand in mine, his skin was so paper thin and so very cold. His eyes were closed and his breathing raspy.

"Ev, I don't think he has long, make any calls you need to," I said.

The doctor and a priest arrived. I had time for the doctor but not for the priest, another one who couldn't meet my eyes. The doctor listened to his heart, took his blood pressure and sadly shook his head at me. No, he didn't have long at all. We made him comfortable and everyone, except me, prayed for him, for his soul. As much as it pained me, I couldn't pray for him because I didn't believe in his God. I watched as Evelyn mumbled her words, her fingers playing with the cross that hung around her neck.

I felt the most gentle squeeze on my hand from him. His eyes had stayed closed but he knew I was there, and then he went, slipped away and out of pain, to his beloved Maria.

We sat with him for a little while and I held Evelyn to me, letting her cry, stroking her hair and trying to soothe her. I watched tears fall from Travis's eyes and I felt numb. I couldn't cry and for the first time in my life, I wanted to. I wanted to feel those tears leave my eyes, roll down my cheeks but I couldn't make them come, I was totally unable to. I had loved this man like a father and now he too, had left me.

I sat in his summer room, looking out for hours, undisturbed. I thought back to the day he had found me, rescued me and Travis from a life on the streets. He had been the first adult to care for me, the only adult who had ever hugged me that I had hugged back and I remembered that day. I didn't like to be touched, the only contact I'd had were the beatings. To have someone, especially someone I viewed as my father, pull me to his chest, place his arms around me and comfort me was strange but I had embraced him back. I now wished that I had done that more. I wished that I had told him how important he was to me, how I had loved him. And that feeling came back, that emptiness in my stomach that I had felt when my parents had died. I knew then what it was, it was grief.

No one came and spoke to me. They understood that I needed that time alone to gather my thoughts, to come to terms with losing him. It was inevitable that he would die one day, we all did. I guess I had not thought what affect it would have on me, how it would make me feel, and I felt very alone. It was strange because I still had Travis and Evelyn but Joe had been the only parent I had really known. The one who had brought me up, who had taught me another language, had taught me about his way of life, had trained me to become the man I was. Now he was gone and I mourned him greatly.

Whether my upbringing was right or wrong, he'd had morals, a code of conduct so to speak. He gave and earned respect and taught me some of the greatest lessons I was ever to learn. He gave me the opportunity to become who I was, to be the successful businessman and have wealth. He taught me to respect that success and wealth and to never take it for granted.

His funeral was a lavish affair, just what he deserved. Many people came, some from his past, like Massimo, who had been released from prison for that day, and some from the neighbourhood. The old Jew, Joseph, who he had befriended many years ago and had helped set up in business, Ted and the guys mourned him also. There must have been over a hundred people. Because of the nature of some of the mourners, there was a police presence, something I objected to, an intrusion in the day. Mallory and Jones were there leaning against a car with a sneer on their faces. Jones had a pad and seemed to be writing, perhaps a list of names, I wasn't sure. Whenever one of the many security guys got close enough to see, he whipped it away.

He was buried with Maria and after the coffin was lowered people made their way over to me, offering their condolences. Some I had met, many I hadn't, but all viewed me as his son, his successor, the head of the family. In honour of him, I wore my customary black suit but this time with a red tie.

I remembered a time he would mock me. "Always in black, Rob, you need some colour in your life," he would say, laughing.

I saw Joey standing in the distance, away from everyone and I saw the look of hatred in his face as people filed past me, shaking my hand. I had told Evelyn to invite him, Joe was his father after all but it was his choice to stand on the sidelines. I also noted that Mallory and Jones had spotted that he was not with the main party. At no time had he come close to the grave and I wondered, was he there to grieve for his father or just for confirmation he had died?

A reception was held at the hotel we owned, a private dining room closed off for us. I paid my respects to the older members of the families that had come.

“Robert, can I introduce you to my uncle?” Massimo said.

“Roberto, I am sorry for your loss. Guiseppi was a good man, he spoke fondly of you,” an elderly gentleman replied.

I had learnt from Joe that some of the older members of the family referred to me as Roberto. There was a time when they would not accept a non Italian at the head of a family but trusting Joe and his choices, they christened me with an Italian version of my name. I found it slightly amusing, Travis found it hilarious.

His name was Gianfranco and he had brought his wife, Sofia, with him.

“It is a pleasure to meet you, finally,” I said to him before kissing Sofia on her cheeks.

“And of course, my son Luca and his family,” Massimo added.

I shook the hand of a guy as tall as I was. In another life we could have been brothers, we looked so alike.

“I never had the pleasure of meeting Guiseppi, I hear he was a great man,” Luca said.

“He was, Luca. A great man indeed. Thank you for coming, I know he would have been pleased.”

I sat with them and listened to their stories, how they knew Joe. Sofia spoke no English and it was fortunate that I had, many years ago learnt Italian, partly to be able to talk to Joe without anyone else understanding.

I made my way around the guests, shaking hands, kissing cheeks and listening to each tell their story of their friendship with Joe. I sat for a while with Joseph, he was accompanied by Evelyn.

“Robert, you have done my friend, Joe, proud today,” he said.

“Thank you, Joseph. It’s the least he deserves.”

At one point I tuned out, I just sat and watched the people in that room. Some laughed, regaling each other with stories from the past, some wiped a tear from an eye. Everyone had their memories of Joe and from the snippets of conversations I could hear, he would be sorely missed.

“Ev, when you’re ready to leave, let me know,” I heard Travis tell her and I saw her nod her head.

The day had really taken its toll on her, she had cared for her father and her sister for many years, now they were gone, whether that be physically or mentally. She said she felt a little lost and not sure what to do. I took her hand and after saying our goodbyes we made our way to a waiting car.

“How are you holding up, Ev?” I asked.

“I don’t know to be honest. I feel relieved that he’s out of pain and I feel guilty that I feel relieved,” she answered.

“I know what you mean,” I replied.

I took her hand in mine and we travelled home in silence.

“Can I make you boys something to eat?” she asked as we arrived back at the house.

“I’ll do it,” Travis replied.

Evelyn and I stared at each other before giving in to a small laugh, Travis had never cooked a meal in his life.

“What? I can cook something,” he said, indignant.

We sat around the kitchen table, the same table that Evelyn had sat for most of her life, the same table Joe and I had sat having discussions late into the night and we reminisced. We ate the meal Travis had prepared and for a simple pasta dish, it was surprisingly tasty.

Travis and I stayed at the house for a couple of days until Evelyn finally told us to get back to our apartment, to get back to work. It was what Joe would have wanted, not a long period of mourning.

Life carried on, it had to in his memory and I was more determined than ever to be a success, to build my company in honour of him. We named the park in the New York complex after him, Guiseppi Gardens. I had arranged for a small plaque to be placed on one of the benches, just his name and the years he had been born and died. We sat on that bench for an hour after the opening, just the three of us, watching kids test out the new play equipment, each with our own thoughts and memories. The thing I thought of the most, when I looked at that memorial plague on the bench, was the dash. That little line between the date Joe was born and the date he died. That dash resembled his whole life, his achievements and his family. That dash was more important that the dates themselves.

Chapter Five

The first new company I bought came about more by mistake than anything. I was twenty-seven and until then had been content with what we already had. Richard had been talking about a couple of properties next door to each other, one was an empty warehouse and the other a manufacturing factory. We decided to take a look at the empty one. The area was mainly industrial but could have good letting potential and in the future, perhaps conversion to apartments. It looked out over the river with good access. The owner was an elderly gentleman, wanting to sell up and cash in his pension.

Next door was a larger warehouse and I wanted to know more about it. We found out that the company had four shareholders, one main and three smaller ones. It was just about breaking even with no real profit and no future but the site was good. We quietly approached each of the smaller shareholders offering them a good price for their shares until we then owned the majority. Now all we had to do was persuade the larger shareholder to sell up. Not something that he wanted to do initially.

In the end he had no choice, I had put Richard in there temporarily and we eased him out. I paid him a fair price for his shares, perhaps a little more than they were worth and closed down the manufacturing. It was hard to put people out of work, but the property had more value than the business itself and it wouldn't have been long before the business would have to close anyway. We sold off all the machinery and eventually some of the land, making a large profit. That deal caught the attention of the financial papers and I experienced my first exposure to the press.

"Rob, take a look at this," Travis had said one day. He was holding a newspaper.

In the financial section was a photograph of me, I was shielding my eyes and leaving a restaurant with a woman. I had to think to remember her name. The article was about Vassago and an up and coming businessman. I had no idea where they had got their information from, they had my name and age correct but no personal details about me. The article questioned how I had started and where my money had come from. The journalist had alluded to crime. I would have to find out about him, who he had been speaking to, to gain what little information he had obtained.

"Famous at last bro," Travis said, waving the article around.

Fame was not something I wanted at all. I didn't need anyone to go poking around in my background, and I had no desire for someone from the past rearing their ugly head.

"Find out who wrote this, Trav. I don't like what he's referring to," I said.

"Already did, someone by the name of Guy Rogers, think he's an independent."

"What do we know about him?"

"I'm working on it but not too much at the moment. Seems to be a bit elusive."

What came from that though were offers, invitations and requests for donations to various causes. I refused most, I wanted a private life and not one in front of the media. However, something had caught my eye one day. It was a request for a donation to a children's home. A blanket letter, probably sent to hundreds of businesses in DC. The home was for children, like Travis and I had been, homeless, who needed shelter and I wanted to know more.

"Trav, what do you think of this?" I asked him, showing him the letter.

"Sounds kind of cool," he replied. "I wonder what would have happened if we had found one of these," he said.

"Well, I doubt we would be sitting here, probably working at the local grocery store now," I laughed.

"Come on, let's go and check it out," I said.

We drove to Arlington and I rang on the way, an appointment was made for us to visit. There was never going to be a refusal, knowing who we were. We arrived at a run-down old house, most definitely in need of a few repairs and with a large garden. We noticed a sign just outside, Stone House, fate perhaps? An elderly woman opened the door and she extended her hand to us.

"Thank you for coming, I'm Nancy, Nancy Pearson," she said.

We followed her into the lounge, again, a room in serious need of redecoration. The ceiling was stained from an old water leak and rivers of condensation ran down the windows soaking into the rotten frames. Although the house was clean and tidy, it was clear it would need some money spent on it.

"Tell me, Nancy, about the home," I asked.

"It started out as my family home, my parents died a long time ago and as time went on I got a bit lonely I guess. A couple of lads used to knock on the door, wanting jobs, mow the lawn and such, and I realised they were homeless. I felt sorry for them and occasionally I would feed them, let them stay. I liked their company. They stole from me, obviously," she said with a chuckle.

"But I thought, I had this big old rambling house, why not open it officially as a home. I have all the registration papers, it's all in order. What I don't have, Mr. Stone, is enough money to keep it going. The state provides some, but it's never enough," she added.

We took a walk around. The house had six bedrooms, two lounges and a large kitchen diner. There was a porch area to the back of the property and a good couple of acres of garden. It needed a new roof, some new windows and most certainly a lick of paint. I met a couple of the kids who were staying there, they were clean and respectful. A social worker came weekly to check on them and Nancy made sure they went to school.

"Do you know how many children are homeless in this city?" she asked, showing us around.

"Thousands. It's disgusting that in these days children are still on the streets, especially in one of the richest countries in the world," she said, shaking her head in anger.

A look passed between Travis and I. Arriving back in the house, we settled in the kitchen with a cup of coffee and a plate of homemade cookies.

"Do you look after the kids yourself, is there any help?" I asked her.

"I have someone come in and clean but other than that, I do most of it myself," she said.

Without needing to think anymore, I offered her a proposal.

"Nancy, this house needs a lot of money spent on it, repairs, redecoration and some modernisation," I said, looking around the out dated kitchen.

"We want to buy this house from you. It will stay as a home and I would like for you to stay here, but with help. You already have a good way with the kids and I think it would be important for you to continue to live here."

"We'll have the house valued and give you a fair price for it," Travis added.

Without hesitation she agreed and we arranged for our lawyer to contact her with all the details. I don't think her fund raising had gone too well and this was probably the best offer she was ever going to get.

As we left Travis said, "Rob, let's do this together, just you and me. Keep it outside of Vassago, this is personal," and I agreed.

We made the purchase and organised the renovations. It was hard going, renovating a building with as little disruption to the kids as possible, but we ended up extending the property a little. We made ten bedrooms, all en suite and one with its own lounge area for Nancy. We installed a new kitchen and larger dining area, one large lounge, an office and a room for the social workers to use, a private space for any therapy that was needed.

The grounds were reorganised, lawned to create play spaces and although a boundary fence was erected we didn't want gates. We wanted the kids to be able to walk in from the street. We met with the social workers and explained what we were doing, how we would take on 12 kids at a time and best of all, Evelyn wanted to be involved.

"Rob, I would like to do something at the home, maybe I can help cook and clean," she said when we had told her about it.

"Sure, if you want to. However, we plan to put in a manager, the kids need a male presence as well, someone who will be tough but fair with them," I replied.

Maria had been placed in a home, her dementia getting bad and Evelyn felt like she rattled around her house with no purpose. She wanted to help Nancy and between them they would make a fantastic team. However, there was one other person I wanted on board, someone I thought would be great, especially for the boys, so I called him.

"Ted, I have a little project I want you to be involved in."

"Sure, Rob, anything for you. Now, tell me all about it," came his reply.

The boxing club had been closed down a long time ago and although we made sure Ted had a flat of his own, he was lonely and bored. Some of the kids would need a bit of tough love and I wanted a man about the house. I wanted the kids to have a balanced upbringing.

Once the works were complete and the home 'reopened' we had six boys, two per bedroom and two girls. We had a set of rules documented and each child had to sign one and keep a copy, a kind of contract between them and us. Rule number one was to always feel that they could talk openly about how they felt. They had their games, their toys, electronic stuff and if anyone broke something through neglect, it would not get replaced. I wanted them to learn to respect what they had. Each had little jobs to do for which they would get a weekly allowance, although we monitored what they spent it on. They needed to learn to handle money, to spend wisely or to save for their future. And that's what the home gave them, a future.

Travis and I would go there once a fortnight, meet with the kids, listen to them and just chat about what they had been up to. We made sure they went to school, they saw the doctor when necessary and we helped them to prepare for later life. As they got older, some went on to college, some we found jobs for and some would just disappear, maybe we would hear from them occasionally, others we wouldn't.

Evelyn went to the home every day, she cooked and supervised. She had a cleaner and a kitchen helper and of course Ted, who had moved in after Nancy decided she wanted to retire. Ted was amazing with the kids, although an old man, he was still strong, still fit enough to separate a scuffle every now and again. He was someone the kids respected because he understood them. He got how hard their life had been and although he was tough, he was a fair man.

I'd missed Ted and although Travis and I still worked out, I missed the old club. We decided to turn the basement of the office building into a gym, install some high tech equipment and a boxing ring. Neither Travis nor I had fought for years, we had no need, but I wanted to get back in the ring, just for old times' sake.

I also wanted for the kids to experience what we'd had. Being in the boxing club, all those years ago, had taught us some discipline and how to defend ourselves. Although I didn't want to promote violence, I wanted them to have the confidence that came with the knowledge that they could protect themselves if needed.

It was agreed that the staff could use the gym, each given a pass but one night a week it was strictly for the kids. A way of ensuring they got some exercise to keep them healthy and a night out, away from the TV and the games.

"Come on bro, let's see if you've lost your edge," Travis joked on the day it was completed.

"Trav, I could still knock you into next week," I replied.

"Yeah, yeah, keep dreaming."

We changed into some workout gear and warmed up, pounding away at the heavy bag, the speed ball and eventually getting in the ring. Ted and the guys were watching, we had been formidable fighters at one time and we had fun, pounding away at each other. It was a good way to release some stress and tension from the day. I still had this compulsion to hurt people, my way of paying back society for what it had done to me, but I was a much more controlled person now.

"Come on, Mack," Travis called out.

"Trav, last time I was in a ring, you were still in short pants," he replied, laughing.

We enjoyed ourselves, we laughed and Travis mocked me about the 'groupies' as he called them who had come to test out the gym. Perfectly made up women in the skimpiest of clothing sashayed past us, trying to get noticed. I watched Travis as his eyes followed one, giving me the chance to get a punch to his head.

"No fucking the staff," I said as he turned his face towards me.

****

Travis and I still dated, him more than me and it soon became awkward. I hated waking up in the mornings and having some half naked female wandering around the apartment or draped over the sofa drinking my coffee, eating my food. As I got older, the more private I became and for good reason.

I still had this fear of anyone knowing what we had done in the past, what I had done and with Travis having girls back all the time, I began to feel exposed. I didn't want these people in my private space, knowing anything about us. I decided it was time to move out of the apartment.

"Trav, we have to talk about our living arrangements," I said.

"What's up?" he asked.

"I don't like bringing girls back here, I don't like how often you do. We need to have our own private space. We keep the apartment, a fuck pad, but let's move, get a proper house," I said.

"Ooh, listen to you, Mr. All Grown Up," he laughed.

"I'm serious, you're a messy fucker. I want to build something, outside the city."

"Okay, but that's not going to happen overnight, is it?" he replied.

"No, so in the meantime we're moving into this."

I showed him the details of a house Vassago had just taken over. It was a large house that the company had already remodelled. There was a spacious kitchen, dining room, four bedrooms with en suite and dressing rooms and two lounge areas. I loved living with Travis, I had since I was eleven and I wanted to share a house, but I also wanted my own space. We were twenty-nine years old, at some point we had to cut that string that bound us.

Travis dated women like they were going extinct, one night it would be the blonde, the next the brunette. His old bedroom in the flat seemed to be getting more action that it had when we lived there. I had been dating Nikki for a little while. She was nice enough and I enjoyed her company. She had a good job, her own place but after a few months she got restless with our relationship, she wanted more. She constantly asked why she was never invited to my home, why I never took her with me to the functions I had began to attend. She wanted the fairy tale ending, to marry the millionaire, the most eligible bachelor in Washington according to some newspaper or another. Occasionally we would be photographed together and she would love it, I would hate it.

It came to a head one day. In her bathroom I found her birth control pills, I noticed that she hadn't taken any for a while and I was fucking livid. The last pill taken had been on a Sunday according to the packet and five days had passed.

"What's this?" I asked her as I stormed back into the bedroom, throwing the packet at her.

She looked shocked at my discovery. "I don't know what you mean?" she stammered.

"You have taken yourself off the pill, haven't you? Do you think if you fell pregnant I would be pleased about it?"

I calculated we had only had sex twice in that week and I prayed that she wasn't. I had decided a long time ago I would never father a child. I never wanted to bring a child into this world and I knew I would not be a good dad. To have someone as innocent as a child in my life, terrified me.

"So I may have missed a day or two, it's no big deal, Robert," she had replied.

"No big deal, are you kidding me?" I asked, stunned.

"Do you love me? Do you have any feelings for me at all? You spend one or two nights a week here, you don't take me to your own home or introduce me to your friends. What is this?" she asked, waving her hand between us.

"It is what it is, Nikki. I've never lied to you, I've never promised you more. I can't give you what you want," I said.

"You can't or you won't? There is a big difference. Robert, you're going to end up very lonely, you know that don't you?"

Her comment pulled me up short. She was right but then I just didn't know how I could change that. I had my friends, but I did crave a relationship. I wanted to arrive home each evening to a woman I was so desperately in love with. I wanted to sleep the night with someone in my arms, who I would miss each moment we were apart. But somewhere in my brain I felt I didn't deserve that happiness so I shut down. I wouldn't let myself love anyone, other than my friends, because I thought, somewhere down the line, they would leave me.

I walked away from her, I would never see her again because I couldn't trust her. She was willing to get herself pregnant deliberately to trap me into a relationship I didn't want. That was a problem I found a lot. Women wanted more than I was willing to give, was able to give. I was too damaged, too mistrustful. They all wanted the fairy tale ending but, in my mind, there was no Fairy Godmother and I was definitely no Prince Charming.

"Hi, Rob, are you hungry?" Evelyn asked when I returned home. She came over, as she had always done, every day to make sure we had a meal and to look after the house.

"What's wrong?" she asked, seeing the anger in my face.

"Fucking Nikki, that's what's wrong," I told her what had happened. Along with Travis, she was the only person I spoke about my private life to.

"Rob, what do you expect? She loves you, she wants a proper relationship, it's not so terrible you know," she said.

"Ev, you and Travis, you don't get it. I don't want that. I don't want people to know who I really am, what I was, and look at me Ev, what kind of father would I make," I said.

"A good one, if you ever let yourself," she replied. "You are not responsible for your past, only your future. And that future can only be what you make it."

I shook my head. "You don't understand. Other than for you and Travis, I don't feel anything, for anyone. What would happen, Ev, if she had got pregnant, I held that baby in my arms and didn't feel anything for it?"

Evelyn came towards me, placing a hand on my cheek.

"You can't know what you would feel, Rob. However, it would help if you loved the mother so this Nikki isn't the one. Who knows what's round the corner for you. Just try not to close yourself off from love," she said.

I shook my head. I knew both her and Travis worried about me, they tried really hard to make me have some kind of normal life but having lived the way I had, done the things I had done, that was impossible. That fear of my past catching up with me, the fear of rejection, kept me alone.

****

I was alerted by Paul to a piece of land in Great Falls, a wooded, rural area, named after its waterfalls and outside of Washington. He knew I was looking for somewhere to build my house and we took a drive out to view it. It was perfect, a six acre plot surrounded by woodland. Just the right amount of privacy for me but with only a half hour drive back into the city. The plot had a few small stone buildings and a chapel. At first I had wanted the chapel torn down, it was not a place I was comfortable having around. That was until I walked in. The door was broken and it took a few pulls to gain access but once I did, staring straight at me was a cracked and dirty, stained glass window.

That window sent a shiver up my spine and it stopped me in my tracks. Paul and Travis had walked in behind me and silently we all looked at the angel, God above, casting her away. The angel was a replica of the tattoo I had on my back, yet that tattoo had been done years before, and I had been the one to draw the design. She had the same long black hair, the sad face and her arms outstretched.

"Leave this building standing, Paul," I said quietly, as I made my way out.

"Do you want anything done with it?" he asked.

"No, just fix the door so no one can get in."

It was not just the window that had disturbed me, it was the sense that the building would mean something to me one day. It had a purpose that I was yet to grasp. I just knew that in the future, that building would be important. I took a walk around, studying the inscriptions on the headstones to the side. Young men, women and children who had died centuries ago lay to rest under my feet. No, there was no way I would disturb that place.

I had one of our architects draw up plans. I wanted the living space on the top floor with glass walls, I still had to have that connection with the outside, and no blinds at the windows. I wanted it open plan, to have a feeling of space not confinement. I wanted it modern, not too much furniture and I also wanted somewhere for Travis and Evelyn to live.

It was time for Travis to live on his own. I was going to have to force the issue a little, as much as he wanted me to have a normal life, I wanted the same for him. By living on his own, he might feel he was able to do that but I still wanted him close.

A garage complex with two large apartments above, next to the house, would give us all the separation I thought we needed. But the thought that we were just a short walk away from each other suited us all.

Evelyn had already started to talk about selling the house, the one she'd inherited from Joe. It was too large for her, she was finding it a struggle to manage the house, the kids' home and looking after us and I wanted to start to make life a little easier for her. She never wanted for anything, she was a wealthy woman in her own right, she had the money Joe had left and I made sure she had whatever else she needed.

So I sat them down and outlined my plans.

"Trav, it's about time you had your own place, you can keep it as messy as you like and it won't stress me," I said.

"This looks great, Rob. When does the building start?" Travis asked, running his eye over the drawings on the kitchen table.

"The sale of the land should go through in a week or so. Then we can get started."

I had thought about building a couple of houses, but knowing Travis, he was comfortable in an apartment, he didn't want to rattle around a house. To soften the blow somewhat I had bought Travis and I a present, something I had taken a lot time to organise and had shipped to the US.

Travis was a speed freak, he was the one who always wanted to drive, he hated to be a passenger and I was happy to be driven. Just occasionally I got the buzz, the need to let rip and drive as fast as I could and I had found the perfect machines for that.

"Come on, I want to show you something," I said.

We headed outside to the garages. Opening them, standing in the middle, gleaming and brand new were two identical black Ducati motorbikes. Fast, powerful, sleek, a perfect representation of us, I thought.

Travis and I had learned to ride bikes years ago. It was when he had smashed up the latest of many cars because of his reckless driving and as a punishment, Joe had made us ride a bike. I think he thought we would be scared but the total opposite happened. We loved it. The excitement of racing a bike through the city, weaving in and out of the traffic, to open up the engine on a long stretch of road with no helmets and the wind stinging our faces was pure heaven to me, and total freedom. Just man and machine.

"Oh fuck, Rob, where did you get them?" he asked.

"Rome believe it or not. Remember Luca, Massimo's son? He has a contact. Come on, let's go see what these beauties can do."

"Boys, helmets please," Evelyn said.

Donning two black helmets we sat astride the bikes, pushed the button for the engine to start and revved. The noise was immense, a growl that echoed around the garage. Wheel spinning out and kicking up dust and stones, we headed off into the night to test out the bikes. We raced each other and had fun, something I hadn't done for a very long time.

We flew through the night like bats out of hell, scaring the shit out of anyone we came across, enjoying the ride.

"Fuck me, that was amazing," Travis said as we pulled into a roadside café.

"They're something else, aren't they?" I replied.

Taking a table outside, Travis and I sat for a coffee.

"You okay about this move?" I asked him.

"Sure. I guess it's time to grow up a little," he laughed.

"Seriously bro, I'm looking forward to it. People will talk if we continue to live together," he added with a wink.

****

The house took just under a year to build, it was to be my first real home, one I designed and knew I would live in for many years. I hated moving about, I wanted something steady, something constant and my own home was going to be it.

The plans would change frequently, especially if Travis was involved, but eventually it got done. The whole place was fixed up with the latest security measures with cameras inside and outside the house. Each car was fitted with a sensor allowing it to pass through the gates and the whole security system was linked to the one at the office so it could be monitored twenty-four hours a day. I had an intercom fitted, we could communicate between us and I wanted the wooded area around the grounds to be left as they were. A perfect shield but also one of the places I always felt most comfortable in. Walking around the woods one day, after a site visit, I took out my keys and carved two initials in a tree, C and R. A replica of a carving from years past and a reminder of how far I had come.

Travis's suggestion was a shooting range. We had licensed guns, everyone did, and he wanted somewhere we could practice. We did this in the woods near one of the little stone buildings that still stood, a perfect gun room.

The day we moved in was probably one of the best I'd had. It was nice to be able to walk around in my own space with none of Travis's mess. I stood at the window as the night drew in, a glass of wine in my hand marvelling at how far I had come. Just turned thirty-two, more money than I could ever spend in my lifetime and a wonderful home. Not a house, for the first time in my life, I had a home.

That first night I slept so well. I had thought I might not, this being the first time I'd slept in a house alone but I loved the quiet. I loved the fact that I could lie in bed and watch the sun rise, no blinds at the windows and no one could see in but I still had that connection to the outside.

No one would visit, I didn't want that. I wanted total separation from my work life, my, although not wanted, public life and my private life. Only here I could be me. Listening to music was what I did most. I'd never really watched TV, although I had one installed in its own room, but to sit and listen and think and not have to talk was my idea of bliss. I was more than comfortable with my own company, unlike Travis who, at first, struggled living on his own.

He would often pop over, help himself to a beer and flop on the sofa. As much as I still enjoyed his company the fact that he quickly grew bored listening to music meant he left earlier and earlier to watch the crap he was addicted to on TV.

"There's a game on," he would say.

"So go watch it then," I replied with a smile.

"You got old quick," he would grumble as he left, flipping me the finger when I laughed.

"No, bro, I grew up, big difference," I called out to his retreating back.

For the next couple of years I became more settled, the business was doing well. There was talk of a possible recession, America was finding itself up against its banks. So I decided to invest some of the company's wealth in gold, then at a low but with predictions for an increase in value. Not that I was too concerned, but much of the company's wealth was in property and we were starting to see a fall in value. Most of what we owned was leased out so a fall in value was not going to hit us as hard, but I would need to keep an eye on the development side. Again, I thanked my good instinct.

As the price of gold soared and property values fell, the company became wealthier than it had before. More and more people were looking to rent instead of buying and we found ourselves in a situation with prospective tenants waiting for a vacancy. Building costs lowered and we took advantage of that. As the recession deepened, we became stronger, more profitable and we were able to give something back. We were able to invest, to give loans to companies. It was slightly ironic that we, in a small way, headed back in the direction we had come from.

Chapter Six

I took a call from my PA, Gina, as I was looking through some papers.

"Mr. Stone, I've just been told that Miranda is on her way up. Are you free to see her or shall I tell her you're busy?" she asked.

I rolled my eyes. I had got to know Miranda after getting involved with a fund raiser at the Smithsonian Museum a few months back. We had been out for meals, I'd taken her back to the apartment after and, as usual, she was getting pushy, wanting more.

"Fine, send her in," I sighed.

The problem I had was that Miranda was Gina's friend. It was at a business function that Gina had first introduced us.

"Robert, it's good to see you," she purred as she walked into my office.

She was dressed in a red wrap around and dangerously high heels. As much as she irritated me, I felt a twitch in my pants.

"What can I do for you, Miranda?" I asked.

"I just wondered if you had time for lunch? I haven't heard from you this week and I was in the neighbourhood," she lied, she was never 'in the neighbourhood'.

I looked at my watch. I should be concentrating on work, I should be telling her that I wasn't interested but my cock overruled my brain. I stood from my desk and walked towards her. I watched her pupils dilate, her tongue run across her upper lip yet she took a step back, away from me.

"I have half an hour," I said.

I walked to the office door, towards the elevator. She followed. We stood in silence as we travelled one floor up, to the apartment. I took the key from my pocket and opened the door, stepping to one side to allow her to enter. The least I could do was to be well mannered. She walked to the centre of the lounge, keeping her back to me. I watched her undo the belt at her side and shrug her shoulders, the dress falling to the floor. She slowly turned. She wore black lace panties and a matching bra. I strode towards her, taking her face in one hand turning it to the side giving me access to her neck.

I very rarely kissed on the mouth. I guess that was too intimate for me and I didn't feel the connection with her to want that intimacy. However, my lips trailed a path down the side of her neck and across her shoulder. I heard her breath quicken, I felt her hands on my chest, loosening my tie. I pulled her bra down, releasing a breast and sucked on her nipple while she fumbled with the zipper on my pants.

Her hand closed around my cock, squeezing and pumping as I hooked my fingers in the side of her panties. They tore away easily enough, the delicate lace having no resistance. Holding her by the hips, I turned her away from me, pushing her until she was bent over the back of the sofa. I reached under her, teasing her clitoris, feeling her tremble at my touch. I listened to her moans of pleasure as I brought her to an orgasm. As she recovered, I pushed into her. I held her hips as I fucked her from behind. She pushed back against me, forcing me deeper and deeper with every thrust.

I reached around her side, clamping a nipple between my thumb and forefinger. I twisted and tugged, harder as her moans increased. I wrapped my other hand in her hair, pulling her head up.

"Fuck me, harder," she said.

Miranda liked it rough. She often came to me already bruised and with broken skin across her back. I could still see the faint handprint sized markings on her ass from whoever she had been with, probably just a few days ago. We weren't exclusive which always made me wonder why she pushed for a relationship with me.

Letting go of her now tender nipple I ran my hand over her pussy, back up, spreading her juices over her ass. I slowly pulled out of her. She knew what was coming next, I watched her grip the edge of the sofa and spread her legs further. I ran my hands over her ass cheeks, spreading them before running the tip of my cock over that one place I knew would send her wild. Did I do this for my pleasure? Not really, it was more for a sense of power, I was claiming a part of her body.

"You want this?" I asked.

"Yes, now," she demanded.

"What do you say?" I asked.

"Please, Robert, fuck my ass."

So I did. She screamed out my name as she came. As I was about to give in to my release, I pulled out of her, my come pumping onto her ass cheeks.

I stood and took a step back, I watched her legs tremble and her breathing start to slow. I pulled my shirt over my head, undid my pants and walked to the bathroom. I needed to shower, not just to clean myself but to also rid my body of the scent of her. I had finished my shower as she walked, naked but carrying her clothes, into the bathroom. I exited the shower, leaving it running for her.

"All yours," I said as she passed.

Heading to my closet, I pulled off the rails a clean shirt and tie, a fresh suit. I was sitting at the small table in the kitchen, tapping my foot impatiently when she returned.

"Are you busy later?" she asked, still standing as I hadn't invited her to sit.

"Yes," I replied.

I stood and made for the door, holding it open so she could leave. I needed to get back to work. The elevator doors opened and I placed my hand on her back, ushering her in. Just as it closed she turned to me. She placed one hand on my chest, the other around the back of my neck, raising herself to kiss me. I moved my head, her lips just catching the side of my cheek.

"You are one mean bastard," she said.

"So I've been told, many times," I whispered as my teeth bit down hard on her earlobe.

The door opened at my floor and I walked out without a backward glance. I saw Gina glance up, her eyes dart between me and her friend, an uneasiness in her look. I heard the elevator doors close and I settled back at my desk to continue my day. I chuckled as I recalled her comment. 'One mean bastard' was probably one on the tamest things she had called me over the past few months.

"What are you laughing at," I heard Travis say as he entered the room.

"Just had a session with Miranda," I said.

"What did she call you this time?" he asked with a laugh.

"A mean bastard. Pretty nice for her."

"I really don't know why you go there," he said, shaking his head.

"Neither do I. It was a cock over brain moment," I replied, picking up my papers.

Miranda and I had a very toxic *relationship*. As much as she pushed for us to be together, I doubted she liked me very much. She wanted the publicity that came with being with me, nothing more. I decided that I didn't need that toxicity in my life at that point. I had enough stress with the business, without Miranda adding to it. I sent her a text.

"That was the last time."

"You say that now," she replied.

"I mean it. Don't push me."

She didn't reply but I had no doubt that wouldn't be the last I would hear from her. All I wanted was to concentrate on a rather difficult takeover I was caught in the middle of, an ailing business that had defaulted on its loan payments to Vassago.

Chapter Seven

Travis had fallen in love. He spent days telling me all about her and I was, at first, genuinely pleased for him. I would watch from the house as he took one of the cars from the garage, dressed in a suit and tie for his date. By the time he had seen her constantly for a month, I knew he probably was, in love. It was unusual for Travis to date someone for that length of time, even more so to see them nearly every night of the week. Previously, he would declare his undying love after a couple of days of good sex then get bored two or three weeks later.

"Mack, keep this between us, but check out this woman," I said as I handed him a note with her name written on.

"Travis's new woman?" he asked.

"Yes, just want to be sure, you know?"

He nodded as he left. I felt it was important to know the background of not just our employees but the people we dated as well. I remembered the Evelyn and Carlo situation and I wanted to be sure the same wouldn't happen to Travis. There was one thing that was making me a little uneasy though. Although he hadn't mentioned it, I wasn't sure that I would be comfortable if she visited him at his apartment. I guess he had every right to take her home but having a stranger around didn't sit well with me.

"Me and Shelly went to the club last night," Travis told me when he had returned to the office.

"Nice meal?" I asked, looking up from my papers.

He certainly had it bad. He told me what she had ordered, how she ate, the delicate way she dabbed her napkin to her mouth even. I smiled and nodded along, pleased for him. But I was also aware that he was telling me inconsequential things, perhaps he was building up to asking something. I wasn't ready for that and thankfully the phone rang on my desk cutting short our conversation.

"Yes," I said.

"Got what you asked for but I see you have Travis with you," Mack replied.

My office, as with the rest of the building, had concealed cameras which fed a live link direct to the office Mack sat in.

"Okay, give me ten minutes or so," I replied.

"I'm heading for the deli, you want me to pick you something up?" Travis asked.

"Sure, whatever you're having will be great," I replied.

With Travis gone, I made my way to the next office.

"Mark, take a break for ten minutes," Mack said to the guy beside him.

I took his vacated seat and Mack opened a file on the desk.

"A couple of concerns. She told Travis she was the manager at a restaurant but she's just a waitress and she has a lot of debt," he said.

"What kind of debt," I replied, this piece of information was important.

"Rent arrears, utilities, car payment," he listed off the amounts.

"Think she's looking for a meal ticket?" I asked.

"Mmm, possibly. What do you want to do?"

"Nothing, I won't interfere, not yet. He's a grown man and I guarantee if that's what she's after, he'll pick up on that."

Travis wasn't a dumb man, he was more than aware of the many gold diggers that had come and gone. I just wanted to be sure there was nothing I needed to worry about and it pained me to do that to Travis. He would know that I would check, we did with everyone we came in contact with and perhaps that was the reason he had told me her full name, told me information about her. Perhaps he already knew what Mack had found out. He had done the same for me in the past. In that office was a cabinet with files on everyone we had dated over the years.

****

I picked up the telephone that had started to ring on my desk.

"Mr. Stone, I have Luca Gioletti on the phone for you, shall I put him through?" Gina said, as I answered.

"Yes, put him through."

I waited for the connection.

"Luca, it's good to hear from you," I said.

"Robert, thanks for taking my call. I wanted to speak to you about your new development if you have the time?" he asked.

"Of course, what do you need to know?" I replied.

The development he was referring to was our third over the years in Manhattan and was to be the largest. A complex of apartments, restaurants and high end boutiques framing a courtyard.

"We would like to buy some of the apartments, off plan of course. However, I would like to make an offer. We supply the labour in return for the apartments," he said.

"An interesting offer, Luca, but I do have my own teams of labour, as you well know."

"But not based in New York. Using mine would certainly make things easier for you. I have some terms drawn up and would like to send them over, for your consideration."

"Of course. I'll need to run them by the board you understand. Send them over and I'll get back to you in a week or so. Now, how are your family, your father?" I asked.

"The family are good, our lawyers are looking at negotiations with our friends for an early release for dad," he replied.

"That's good news, give him my regards when you speak to him next."

We said our goodbyes and I sat and looked at the phone for a little while. That was an unusual request. I knew Luca's family were not as cash rich as ours and perhaps the offer of his labour was because he couldn't afford to outright buy my apartments, but I would look through his proposal and run it by the team, as promised. Over the years I had began to distrust Luca, not that anything he did had an impact on me but rumours were rife that he was under investigation by our 'friends' the FBI, and I wasn't about to get pulled back into a lifestyle I had spent years shedding.

I had much respect for his father and his great uncle, Gianfranco. They reminded me of Joe, old school and well respected. Luca, however, was a different man altogether. Because of the development it was beneficial to maintain a professional friendship though.

"Lunch," I heard Travis say, as he walked through the office.

"Thanks. I just had an interesting conversation," I replied, telling him about the call.

"I wonder what he's up to?" Travis said.

"No doubt we'll find out soon enough."

His phone beeped alerting him to the fact he had received a text message, his smile broadened as he read.

"You need me for anything? That was Shelly, she wants to meet," he asked.

I shook my head. "Mark can run me home."

He left the office, replying to his message. I sat for a while thinking. I really hoped this relationship would work for him. I certainly hadn't seen him smile so much. He hadn't been gone ten minutes when I received a call that the girlfriend was in the foyer. Wondering what she could want with me, I told security to send her up. I had been approached in the past by one or two of his girlfriends, mainly for advice. He was as difficult as I could be sometimes. I wasn't really able to give relationship advice so often just diverted them back to him.

I watched a blond in a skirt too short and a top too tight walk across to announce her arrival to Gina. I frowned, this was not

Travis's usual. And since Travis was on his way to meet his girlfriend I began to wonder who this woman was.

I picked up my phone and called through to Mack while she waited in my reception.

"Take a look at the camera, is this woman Shelly Masters?" I asked.

I heard a rustle of papers. "Yes, fits the photo I've got, although she certainly looks a lot trashier in the flesh," he replied.

Placing the phone back on the desk I nodded through the glass to Gina. Shelly was shown into my office. The very first thing I noticed was an overpowering smell of cheap perfume. She stopped midway across the room.

"Robert, it's a pleasure to finally meet you," she said.

"What can I do for you?" I asked without any real pleasantries.

With that she moved towards my desk, I assumed to sit at one of the chairs. Instead she perched on the edge, angling her body towards me. Her already short skirt had risen and her shirt strained against her breasts.

"Isn't Travis on his way to meet you?" I asked.

"Yes, I just wanted five minutes to meet the secretive Robert Stone," she replied.

"Well, now you have. Perhaps you should get going," I said, standing from my chair.

"Oh now, don't be mean." At least she had the grace to look a little nervous as she spoke.

"You haven't seen me mean. I recommend that you don't," I replied, taking a step towards her.

"I like a mean man, Robert. Someone as powerful as you is a real turn on."

I glanced up at the camera in the corner, checking the little red light was on ensuring this was being recorded.

"You're coming on to me?" I asked, a little stunned and trying to swallow down the anger that was rising.

"If you want me to," she replied with as much sultriness as she could muster.

"Get the fuck off my desk. You are dating my best friend and you walk in here, looking like a cheap whore and coming on to me?"

Her smile faded and she closed the legs she had slid apart earlier.

"I, err, I just thought..."

"You just thought, what? I'd be interested in you. I'll repeat myself. You. Are. Dating. My. Best. Friend." I growled.

She finally slid of my desk and moved towards the door of the office. I noticed her hands shake and I didn't give a fuck if I had scared her. I was livid, I was more than livid, I was sad for Travis. That piece of trash had caught his heart and it was all a lie. I shook my head as she scuttled out, rushing for the elevator.

I saw Mack leave his office, he nodded just the once as he made his way after her. I closed my office door behind me and sat at my desk, slamming my fists on the glass top.

"Fuck," I said to myself.

It wasn't the first time one of Travis's girls had come onto me, but it was the first one he thought he was in love with. I screwed my eyes shut and ran my hand through my hair. What the fuck was I to do? Do I tell Travis and break his heart? Or do I say nothing and hope that was a one off? I checked my watch, he would have got to wherever he had arranged to meet her and found out she wasn't there. The fact that she had lured him away, that level of deceit, made me more angry. I received a text from Mack.

"She's gone to a bar, accepting drinks from a guy next to her. What is more important, the Range Rover is still in the parking lot, I don't know where Travis is," he said.

I frowned and rung down to security.

"Stan, what cars of mine are parked up?" I asked.

"Both, Sir. The Range Rover and the Merc, still in their usual spots," he replied.

"Okay. Did you see Travis leave?"

"He was here just a minute ago, shall I go find him?" he asked.

"No, it's fine, Stan. I'll give him call."

Travis hadn't left the building. Thinking about the time between when he had left and when Shelly had arrived, it could have only been ten minutes at the most, she was probably already waiting outside. But that didn't account for Travis's whereabouts. When Gina returned, I called her into my office.

"Did you see Travis leave?" I asked.

"I didn't, Mr. Stone. I've been in the meeting room, with the PA's for a diary meeting. Is everything okay?"

"Yes, now, grab me a coffee will you?"

It was a half hour later that Travis returned. He had a smile on his face as he came into the office.

"You okay, bro? How was lunch?" I asked.

"Shelly had to cancel, she had a chef throw a fit at the restaurant," he replied.

"Where did you go then?"

"Gym, thought I'd have a quick workout," he said.

I nodded, relieved. For a moment there, I thought he might have seen her come in, seen her lounge over my desk. I wasn't sure what I was going to do, whether to say anything or not but at least I had a bit of time to think. We finished up the day and headed for home.

****

I heard the front door open as I sat on the sofa with my glass of wine, footsteps stomped up the stairs. By the noise I didn't need to look to know it would be Travis.

"Hey, bro," I called out.

He went straight to the kitchen, grabbed a beer before he made his way over, in silence.

"You okay?" I asked.

"Rob, I have a problem, a big problem," he answered.

I sat upright, giving him my full attention.

"What's wrong?"

He reached inside his shirt pocket, pulled out a piece of paper and handed it to me. The page was a standard lined piece of paper, torn from a notebook by the looks of it. As I unfolded it, I watched Travis slump forwards a little, his face in his hands, his elbows resting on his knees. I started to read.

Guess who, brother? I see you've done well for yourself and it's only fair you take care of your family. You fucked off and left us to deal with the shit that was our dad. I bet you don't care but he beat the shit out of Aileen, because of you, then she left. Broke mum's heart, you did. He wouldn't let her come find you and we all paid the price. So, it's only fair you pay now. I know where you are, who you are. Think you're some big shot, huh? Well, brother, time to face the past. I'll be in touch.

Padriac

I read it through, then reread. That had always been his biggest fear, a brother finding out where he was. I sighed, our day was just getting better and better.

"Trav, when and how did you get this?" I said.

He looked up slowly.

"It was on the car windscreen, at the office."

"Why didn't you tell me earlier?" I asked.

We had driven home together. This was the first time he had ever held something back from me and I knew then he was worried and that this was serious.

"I wanted to check it was legit first. Remember I told you how I got here? Aileen is my sister, her boyfriend drove me. I kept my eye on him from time to time, he's a good guy. He called someone who called someone I guess and found out Padriac left New York about a month ago, headed this way."

Travis had never really spoken about his family, this was the first in all the years we had been friends that I was even learning their names. I never pushed for information, it wasn't my place. If he had wanted me to know, he would have told me. However, I was concerned for him. It sounded like simple blackmail and it would need to be dealt with.

"Trav, we need to know what he knows. It might be that we do nothing until he gets in touch again but you need to tell me about your family, so we can prepare. We need the guys in on this as well."

He nodded as he took out his cell phone. He called Mack and asked if he could come over. It was rare that we would call a meeting in the evening, if we did, it always meant there was trouble ahead. Whatever Padriac knew, it would have an impact on all of us. I send a message to Jonathan, Richard and Paul, arranging to meet at the office the following morning. In the meantime, while we waited for Mack to arrive, I headed to the kitchen to grab more beers.

"So, if he put this on the windscreen, he'll be on camera. We can check that out in the morning. In the meantime, do you want Mack to know about your family?" I asked.

He sighed, shrugged his shoulders. "I don't suppose it would hurt. I don't know a great deal but what I do could be a load of lies. My dad was a drunk, my brothers are drunks. I have no idea if what I learnt was a load of bollocks or not. You know, drunken rambling and all that."

"Okay, let me scan this so we have a copy," I said, making my way to the home office.

Before I scanned it I read the note again. The handwriting was messy, although the paper was lined, the words were scrawled across the page haphazardly. Perhaps Padriac had been drunk when it was written. I studied the names, typical Irish names. I remembered that Travis had told me his family had fled Northern Ireland, he said to escape the troubles and settled in New York. This was before he was born. New York seemed a long way to come just to escape the troubles, and I started to wonder exactly what trouble they were running from.

With the note scanned and saved, a copy sent to Mack, I headed back to the lounge. I had never seen Travis look that troubled, there was more to this note and I hoped he would open up to me. He was my brother and I would do anything for him. The Shelly issue would have to take a backseat for the moment, this was more important.

"Rob, there's something else. Padriac didn't just beat Aileen and me," Travis said.

I looked at him waiting for him to continue. He swallowed hard, his gaze fixed on the wall in front of him.

"Remember when we paid your Father Peters a visit?" he said.

"Yes."

"I wanted to deal with Cara's dad for a reason. I never got to pay Padriac back for what he did to Aileen and me."

He didn't look at me when he spoke and I was glad. The realisation of what he was saying shocked me to the core and he would have seen that in my face. Cara had been abused by her father. Travis was telling me his brother had done the same to him. To what extent, I didn't know.

"Do you want to talk about it?" I asked.

"I don't want it going any further than us. Maybe, one day I'll talk about it but not now."

He opened the two beers, my wine now forgotten and as we took the first mouthful the headlights of a car swept across the room as it circled the drive. Looking through the window I saw Mack climb out. Heading to the kitchen for another bottle, I heard him climb the stairs.

"Hey," he called out.

"Beer?" I said, handing him the bottle.

"Sure, what's up?" he asked.

I motioned with my head towards Travis. "We have a problem," I said.

"Girlfriend?" he mouthed and I shook my head.

We made our way back to the sofa where I handed Mack the note. In silence he read, like me a couple of times judging by the time it took.

"Travis found this on the car windscreen earlier tonight, in the office parking lot," I said.

He looked up sharply, his eyebrows raised.

"So we have him on camera then?"

"Yes, we'll check it out tomorrow."

"Trav, do you want to tell us about him?" I asked.

He took a deep breath before he spoke.

"Padriac is the oldest, ten years older than me, I think. After him came Aileen, then Carrig. They were all born in Belfast, I was born in New York. My dad was a drunk, beat us kids and mom. The older boys take after their father. Padriac was the worst, me, mom and Aileen took the brunt of his beatings. He was a prick."

"Aileen left didn't she?" I asked.

"Yes, after I left she headed back to Northern Ireland, stayed with relatives I think. She writes to me every now and again but that's all. I've haven't seen or heard from any of the others," Travis replied.

"We need to find out who knows you're here," Mack said.

"Aileen's boyfriend brought me when I was a kid. He was coming this way and Aileen asked him to bring me, to get me out of the way."

I told Mack what Travis had said previously, about contacting the boyfriend and finding out that Padriac was in DC.

"Well, we need to decide if we wait until he makes contact again or track him down first. I doubt he's going to be a threat physically but do you want someone to shadow you?" Mack asked Travis.

"Fuck no, Mack."

"Could he be dangerous?" I asked.

"I doubt it, Rob. The only worrying thing is what he thinks he knows," Travis replied.

"Okay, we can't do anymore now. I'll get the CCTV up first thing in the morning and we'll talk about it then. You called the guys together?" Mack asked me, I nodded.

I walked Mack down to his car and outside we continued our conversation.

"You tell him about Shelly yet?" he asked.

"No, thought it should wait. To be honest, I don't really know what to say."

"Leave that one to me. I have an idea and it's probably best not coming from you anyway. How's he doing, really?"

"Worried, for sure. This has always been his biggest fear. I want that guy out of the picture, Mack. We can't run the risk of him even hinting he knows anything about us."

He nodded as he got into his car and I walked back into the house. Travis was still sitting in the same position, slumped forwards on the sofa. I took a seat beside him.

"Trav, you know this will get sorted don't you?" I asked.

He looked at me and nodded.

"I don't have any relationship or feelings towards him, Rob. If I catch up with him, he'll wish he hadn't started this. I couldn't give a shit about what he thinks he knows about me, I'm worried about dragging you into this."

"Don't worry about me. We've faced worse than this in the past and no doubt will again in the future. We are brothers, Trav, he's nothing."

Travis finished off his beer and headed off to his apartment. I read through the note one last time before locking it away in my home office and heading downstairs. Standing under the shower, I closed my eyes. When I had asked Travis if he thought Padriac was dangerous, I didn't mean in the physical sense. We couldn't take the risk that he knew anything of our past. No matter how careful we had been, there was plenty that could put us away for a very long time.

I was more concerned, however, about what he would say where Travis and Aileen were concerned. Would he be dumb enough to shout his mouth off when he realised there was no money to be had? As I climbed into bed, my last thought before I drifted off to sleep was of Travis. I pictured him as a little boy, remembering how he looked when I had first met him. No matter what had happened to me physically, he had gone through worse. I didn't want to imagine the horror he and his sister had been subjected to. What I knew was, Padriac would never live to have the opportunity to tell. I would protect my family any way I could.

****

I was up and dressed as Evelyn made her way upstairs. Sipping my coffee, I greeted her.

"Morning, Ev."

"Oh, you startled me. You're up early."

"Early meeting, just waiting on Trav."

"He was in the garage when I came across. Do you want something to eat before you go?"

"No, I'll grab something later. Just another shot of caffeine will do for now," I answered as I placed my cup under the coffee machine.

"You drink too much coffee," she scolded.

I smiled, kissed her on the cheek as I passed to meet Travis. She had always worried, fussed over us and as much as I had told her she didn't need to, it didn't stop her.

"Hey, bro. You okay?" I asked as I crossed the drive.

"Yes, ready to take on the world," Travis replied.

The worried look had been replaced with a look of steel. I climbed in the car and we headed off to the office. I watched as his jaw worked from side to side and knew he hadn't slept a wink. He had closed down. I recognised the look, it was the same I saw for years every time I looked in the mirror. Because of who we were, because of the upbringing we'd had, we understood each other far greater than just friends. But I didn't know how to help him deal with this and he wouldn't want me to try.

Because of the early hour the foyer was empty, save for security, and we travelled up to our floor. Richard, Paul and Jonathan were waiting when we arrived, Mack followed shortly after.

"Thanks for coming in early, we have a problem that I want to discuss with you," I said as we sat on the sofa in my office.

"Yesterday Trav found a note stuck on the windscreen of the car, downstairs in the parking lot. It was a note from his brother, Padriac. A simple blackmail letter by the looks of it."

Mack passed around a copy of the note.

"Mack, what did you find on CCTV?" I asked.

“Excluding security there are three individuals who enter the lot. This one is your man but it’s not a great photo.”

He handed around a rather grainy photograph of a guy, overweight in a dark jacket and with a baseball cap pulled down low to shield his face.

“In the clip he comes into the lot and walks straight to the car. Bearing in mind there are three Range Rovers, he knows which one is yours, Trav. He puts the note under the wiper and walks out, his head bowed so we don’t get a shot of his face at all. Does he look familiar?” Mack asked Travis.

“I haven’t seen him in over twenty years, if he stood in front of me, I probably wouldn’t recognise him.”

“Any logo’s or markings on that jacket?” I asked.

“Nothing, just a plain dark blue probably, jeans and dark shoes. Nothing distinguishable at all,” Mack replied.

“Do you think he knows where the cameras are?” Paul asked.

“Probably, he keeps his head low all the time. The cameras cover the whole lot,” Mack answered.

“So he’s already checked the place out,” Jonathan added.

“I would say that would be a good guess.”

“There’s some things I should tell you, a bit of family history. But first you should know, I have no idea if this is true or not. Paul, you might be interested in this. My parents fled Northern Ireland in the mid seventies with three kids. I was born just after they arrived in New York. They were taken in by a family and for a couple of years they moved around. Remember, I don’t know if this is nothing more than a bit of family folklore. Padriac used to talk about our dad being a butcher, and the reason they fled was because the security forces were after him. He had something to do with the Shankill Butchers, part of the Ulster Volunteer Force and responsible for some horrific deaths. Death by a butcher’s knife.”

“Fuck,” Paul said.

“Exactly,” Travis replied.

Paul had married Rosa, someone he had met on a trip to Southern Ireland, a business trip. Not that Joe had any connections with her family but, if not part of the IRA, they were certainly sympathisers. It was a business deal that Joe pulled out of because he didn't want to deal with the Irish but Paul had come back with Rosa. And because of her heritage, he understood what Travis had told us.

"Although I found all this out just before I left, it wasn't the reason I ran. I wouldn't have been old enough to understand what it meant. No one has ever spoken about it except my sister," Travis said.

"Your sister's back in Ireland isn't she?" Richard asked.

"Northern Ireland, yes. But not Belfast. She's further up country. It's one of the reasons I don't know if it's true. Would she head back to any part of Northern Ireland knowing what her father was involved in?"

"That's a good point. You know, I could speak to Rosa's dad, see if he can find out anymore," Paul said.

"No, thanks though, Paul. I don't think we need to draw any attention to that at all. We have to assume Padriac knows Trav has a bit of money, he might think he knows how he got his money, but no specifics," I said.

I caught movement from the outer office, Gina had arrived. I turned over the papers and photograph we had sitting on the small coffee table between the sofa and chairs as she tapped on the door. She would have seen us sitting there, through the glass wall.

"I'm sorry to interrupt, Mr. Stone, I wondered if you guys would like coffee?" she asked.

"Yes, that would be good," I replied. Travis continued once she had left.

"Anyway, whether it's fact or fiction, Padriac does love to tell a story when he's drunk and he might have run out of an audience for the 'my dad's a Shankill Butcher'. I might be his next source of bar talk," he said.

"To be honest, Trav, him living on an alleged reputation might work in our favour. Who the fuck is going to believe his dad was in the UVF and his brother in the Mafia, that's one unlucky bastard," Jonathan said.

That comment broke the tension in the room and we laughed as Gina brought in a pot of coffee and cups. Once the coffee was poured and she had left, I continued.

"Padriac had left it that he will be in touch although I doubt he'll come back to the lot. He must know we would check the cameras and he has got to be one dumb shit if he does that again. Mack, get hold of Tony, see if we can track him down. My guess is he would hang around the Irish bars if he's a drinker and would probably want to be around his own."

Tony was an investigator we had used on and off over the years. He was especially good at tracking people down and quickly.

"Once we know where he is, we can deal with him," I added.

There was no need to explain what I meant. The guys stood and headed off to start their day. Mack left to contact Tony and Travis and I finished our coffee.

"Didn't get very far, did we?" he said.

"What do you mean?"

"We think we shed our old lifestyle but it's always there, in the background."

"It's not always, Trav. Just every now and again it will rear its ugly head. And you know what, if we didn't have that background we wouldn't be sitting here."

I was surprised by Travis's comment. I was always the one that had pushed for a different life. I had always believed that, if left to Trav, we would still be in that office between the two stores hijacking lorries and God knows what. I chuckled, maybe he had finally grown up too.

It was about midday when Mack called through.

"You're not going to believe this but Tony has a location for Padriac already. Seems he does have a big mouth after all. He was in a bar last night, just around the fucking block. Seems our guy really does have shit for brains. The barkeeper threw him out after he started singing rebel songs."

"So he's staying local then. I've had a thought," I replied.

I ran my thought past Mack before disconnecting the call and getting back to work. Luca had sent through his proposal for our build in Manhattan. He wanted to supply the workforce and instead of payment we would give over some apartments. On paper it didn't seem a bad idea but I would arrange to meet with him and discuss it face to face. He had no idea what my apartments would sell for but I had an idea of build cost so a meeting would start negotiations. He was due to visit DC so I arranged to catch up with him them.

I looked up from my papers as Travis stormed, once more, into my office, he practically fell into the chair opposite my desk.

"Fucking bitch," he said as he flung an envelope down on the desk, gesturing with his hand for me to take a look.

I pulled out a photograph of Shelly sitting on a bar stool, her hand on the thigh of the guy facing her. That guy being someone other than Travis. I sighed, Mack had taken those photos. He had said he was going to deal with it, I hadn't banked on it being right then.

"Shit, bro. I'm sorry. What are you going to do?" I asked.

"Finish it, obviously. She told me she had to cancel our lunch because she was working. She also told me she was the manager of the restaurant, she isn't. We seem to have really lost our edge haven't we? Can't believe I fell for that bullshit."

"Bro, don't beat yourself up over it, these things happen. We've all been there," I said.

He collected up the photographs, stuffed them back in the envelope and as he left the office, he deposited them in the bin. I felt so bad for him. Despite his words, I knew that had cut him deep. I also felt terrible that I hadn't told him the truth. Judging by the photograph and where Shelly had her hand, she wasn't thinking about Travis at all. I placed a call to Mack.

"Talk about kick a man when he's down," I said.

"Didn't happen the way I planned, Rob, sorry. I left that envelope on the desk, he came in and picked it up thinking it was for him, I guess. I told him I'd just collected the post."

"Okay, but let's keep an eye on him right now, he fell hard for that one."

"Where's he gone?" Mack asked.

"Don't know, get a bit of air maybe. I'll give him ten then call him. I fancy a workout, he can take it out on me."

"Good luck with that," Mack said with a chuckle.

Ten minutes later I called him.

"Fancy a hit?" I asked.

"Sure, meet you there."

I made my way down to the basement nodding at one or two people in the elevator as we travelled down in silence. No matter how crowded the elevator got, there was always a little space around me which I was thankful for. I smiled to myself at how uncomfortable some people felt in my presence. I didn't court a friendship with staff, right or wrong, I kept my distance.

"Afternoon, Mr. Stone, here for a work out?" I heard as the elevator doors opened and I stepped out.

"Sure am, Jim. How are you today?" I asked.

I had time for Jim. He was an old guy and had been with us for years. He had started off in security with Stan. I remembered how that came about. Stan had been homeless, he had slept in the doorway. Security never moved him on because in fact, he was like a little security guard himself. He was always gone by morning though. I had worked late into the night and on leaving had seen Jim give Stan some food. My thoughts were immediately taken back to the days when Evelyn used to come find me and Travis with a hot pie and coffee. I had watched for a little while as the two men chatted, overhearing snippets of their conversation. Stan had been in the army, after being injured he had been forced to leave, to live a life on the streets because he had nowhere else to go.

Jim didn't look much better himself. He wore a slightly torn coat, way too thin for the season. As I walked close, I saw Stan try to stand to move off the entrance way. I had told him not to, if he was comfortable there, he could stay. I would make sure security brought him out a coffee. And so it started, each night, these two older men would meet, have a coffee and if it coincided with me leaving, a chat.

Jim was unemployed and it struck me that he was willing to give up part of his living allowance to feed Stan. Once I learnt that, I told them both to come and see me the following day. They started in maintenance until they got a little too old for that. Jim enjoyed working around the gym equipment so he stayed there and Stan sat at the security desk in the foyer, monitoring the coming and goings. Other than my guys, these two were the hardest workers in the whole organisation.

“I'm good, Mr. Stone, you have a good workout,” he said.

I made my way into my changing room and found in my locker my neatly pressed workout clothes. I always started my workout with a run and every running machine faced a bank of mirrors. I liked to scan the room and see what was going on, who was there without catching anyone's eyes directly. I watched as Travis entered, heading for the machine next to mine.

“You're getting a bit loose there, bro,” he said.

“Loose?” I answered.

“Yeah, not as ripped as me anymore. Too much dining out, my friend,” he replied.

I laughed. Travis would never be as ‘ripped’ as he called it, as me. We were two totally different builds. I was pleased to see him smile though, to be back to his usual sarcastic and competitive self. Of course he set his machine to run faster, longer than I did and, as normal, I let him win, until we got in the ring that was.

Wrapping a towel around my neck, I headed over to the ring. Jim secured our gloves and we climbed under the ropes. The usual fan club were working out, always on machines that faced the ring so they could watch. I'd given up a long time ago worrying about them. We sparred for about half an hour, at which point, ‘ripped’ as I called him, was puffing like a train.

We showered, changed back into our suits and headed upstairs. As we walked into my reception, Mack came out of his office with what looked like a photograph in his hand. He nodded his head towards my door.

“Meet your brother,” he told Travis.

The photograph was of an older man, dark hair, unshaven and looking like the drunken bum I was expecting, nothing like Travis at all.

“You sure this is him?” I asked.

"Got the same name, same build as the guy on the CCTV so we're pretty confident. We will know for sure later today but, yes, I think so," Mack answered.

Travis stared at the photo for a while. "You know what, that could be my fucking father standing there. I'm looking forward to meeting him again."

****

"Dinner will be ready soon," I heard as I climbed the stairs to the lounge.

"Thanks, Ev. Smells good."

I took a seat at the breakfast bar.

"Are you okay?" she asked, she had seen me run my hand through my hair, my stress signal

"Travis got a note from his brother, wanting money," I replied.

She stopped stirring whatever was in the pan and looked sharply at me.

"Oh, do you want to tell me?"

"A note was left on the windscreen in the parking lot at work. His oldest brother, Padriac has decided it's time Trav funds his drunken lifestyle. We know where he is, we're going to have a little chat," I said.

She nodded but didn't press any further on the 'little chat'.

"How is he holding up? He told me about Shelly earlier."

"He seems fine with the Padriac thing, but Shelly? I think he loved her and Padriac has come along at just the right time for him to vent a bit of anger."

"You will take care, won't you? With Padriac, I mean."

Evelyn would never ask what my intentions were, she had been brought up in a lifestyle where not knowing everything was the best option. However, she would also understand that Padriac couldn't be allowed to talk. Over the years there had been articles about me but nothing about Travis. It was one of the reasons he never attended events, even if the whole team were invited. As much as I was paranoid about my past catching up with me, Travis was about his family and now I knew why. I didn't want

Padriac shut up because of mine and Travis's past, I wanted him shut up because of what he could say about Travis and Aileen. I had tried, since the previous night, to block any images from my brain, to no avail. I saw Travis in my mind but the feelings coursing through my body were the same as that day, outside the school, in the yard. The last day I ever saw Cara.

"Ev, you know I will. You've got nothing to worry about."

As I poured a glass of wine, she dished up a plate of pasta in a homemade sauce for me, plating some to take to Travis. In the beginning, when I had first moved into the house, Travis would come over and eat. As he got more comfortable living on his own, that started to stop. However, Evelyn just couldn't stop her fussing and if she cooked for me, she always made sure there was enough for Travis.

As I sat on the sofa, my cell started to ring.

"Hi, Mack." I said as I answered.

"We have him. He's staying in an apartment not far from the office. You know that one about ready for demolition? Tony reports that he also drinks in a bar next to it. Seems he hits the bar about lunchtime and staggers out when it closes," Mack said.

"That's great. Have Tony visit the bar, buy him a couple of drinks and see whether it loosens his tongue a bit. You know the drill," I said.

"Sure, I'll have him call me later tonight then."

After I finished the call to Mack, I called through to Travis.

"Think we are on for tonight, bro. You up for this?" I asked.

"Of course, looking forward to it," he replied.

I wasn't sure 'looking forward to it' was the best response but I understood what he meant. Tony would spend some time with Padriac, ply him with whatever he was drinking and see if he could get him to talk. Once he was drunk enough, I had told Mack to get him to the 14th Street Bridge. There was a little spot, beside the river and underneath one of the piers that seemed to be a meeting place for down and outs. Mack would make sure the place was emptied of people before Tony and Padriac arrived.

I sipped my wine, contemplating on what we were about to do. No matter how many times I thought we, as a family, had moved away from these kind of problems, they always seemed to find us. Perhaps I should accept the fact that we would never be the family I craved. Perhaps I should just accept this was my life, I couldn't change it. Yet, this was one 'meeting' that would be totally justifiable.

I received a call just after ten in the evening.

"Hey, our man's going to be moved on soon. He's already upset the bar staff, grabbed one of the girl's on the ass. Tony offered to take him home," Mack said.

"Okay, we'll see you at 14th."

I texted over to Travis and headed down to the bedroom. Putting on a dark coloured pair of jeans and hooded sweatshirt, I made my way outside to climb in the already idling car. Travis was at the rear, attaching new plates. We didn't want anyone to be able to identify the car and trace it back to us. Opening the glove compartment, I checked there were two pairs of gloves.

"Ready?" I asked.

"As always," Travis replied.

I relayed the conversation I'd had with Mack as we made the journey to the bridge. Travis was quiet, his face rigid with tension with just the beat of a pulse at his temple. I understood what he was going through. When we had paid a visit to Father Peters and Cara's family, the memories of that time hit me and were painful. It must be the same for Travis. I didn't know everything that had happened to him, but it had been enough for his sister to want to get him away, to safety. To send him off to a city with no money in his pocket, with nowhere to live and hope that he had the courage and strength to survive, for me, meant his home life had to have been unbearable. I wondered why his sister didn't run too. She was older than Travis, able to care for herself and him. Maybe he'd tell me, maybe not. It was his story and I wouldn't ask, I wouldn't force him to have a conversation if he wasn't ready.

We headed off the road onto a grassy area and stopped the car. With the lights off, the black Range Rover was difficult to see from either the road or by the traffic making its way over the bridge. Walking down the bank and towards the pier, I could make out two figures, one standing and one lying on the floor.

“Robert. Travis, charming brother you have here,” Tony said as we neared.

I chuckled. “What did you get from him?”

“Well, he knows who both of you are and that you have money, Trav. He boasted that his brother owned a big company and that he got his money from crime. He didn’t go into detail and when I asked, he just tapped his nose. He certainly knows, or thinks he knows, something. I didn’t have enough time to get it out of him before he got kicked out.”

“Did anyone around hear him talk?” Travis asked.

“No, the bar was empty and to be honest, the staff pretty much kept away from him. Until he grabbed the waitress’s ass. They hauled him out and left him on the sidewalk.”

“Okay, thanks, Tony. I’ll be in touch,” I said.

That was his cue to leave, he nodded and made his way out. Travis crouched down, looking at the face of his mumbling brother. There was no family resemblance at all. The guy lying on the floor was overweight and stunk of alcohol and piss, the front of his pants stained.

Putting on a pair of gloves, I rifled through the pockets of his jeans, emptying them of the few coins and bits of paper they contained. We rolled him over to check the back pockets for a wallet and his body for any jewellery that could identify him. Finding nothing, we rolled him towards the river. The sound of the traffic above drowned out the noise of him hitting the water and we waited for a while, watching his body float away, face down, from the bank. The cold water revived him though. We stood and watched as his head came up, he spluttered a little as the current started to take him downstream. His arms flailed as he tried to swim back to shore and it was clear swimming wasn’t something he had learnt to do. There was one moment when his face turned towards us. Whether he recognised Travis or not, I couldn’t tell, we were probably too far away and it was too dark. He certainly knew he hadn’t fell though.

He made no attempt to call out, the shock of the cold water rendering him breathless I guess and it wasn’t long before his arms stop trying to drag him against the current. He started to sink beneath the dark water of the Potomac.

We walked back to the car. Without lights, Travis backed the car towards the road, waiting for a clear in the traffic before we heading into town.

“Okay?” I asked.

“Yeah, shame the fat fucker was so drunk. I would have loved for him to have seen my face,” Travis replied.

“Let’s go see what he has in the apartment.”

Pulling up in an alley next to a run-down block, Travis pulled a small pistol, fitted with a silencer from under the seat of the car and fired it at the only streetlight, plunging us and the car into darkness. I looked at him and shook my head.

“You could have just thrown a fucking stone,” I said.

“Not as much fun, bro,” he replied.

We made our way to the front entrance. At this time of night the street was empty of people, this wasn’t a neighbourhood for taking a walk in. Gaining access was easy, the front door was so battered it couldn’t close. It looked like someone had used their boot to gain access recently. Tony had already informed Mack of the apartment number and we climbed the stairs to the top floor. Stepping over soiled diapers and used needles we reached the apartment door. Travis picked the lock and we silently entered. Although Tony had located the apartment we had no idea if Padriac was occupying it alone.

Silently we walked through the rooms. The kitchen sink was full of empty take out containers and dirty dishes. The scuttling of something across the kitchen counter just about summed up the place. There was a mattress on the floor in the bedroom, a towel was nailed to the window to block out the light and overturned beer bottles littered the floor. I rummaged through a small pile of clothes, checking pockets and finding nothing. We then headed to the lounge. On a small wooden table we found a pad, the jagged edge showing where a page had been torn out. Travis put that in the small bag he had produced from his pocket. There was very little furniture just a sofa, a sideboard with empty drawers and the table without any chairs. The furniture looked like it had been abandoned by the previous tenant.

“Sure knows how to live well, doesn’t he?” I whispered.

Travis chuckled. “Reminds me of my childhood home.”

“We moved from dump to dump when I was a kid. This looks like a luxury apartment compared to some of the places we called home. Mind you, mom would scrub the place from top to bottom every day,” he said.

We found nothing of use at the apartment and after making sure the door was closed behind us, we made our way to the car, hoping it still had its wheels. Arriving home, we put back the correct plate on the Range Rover and headed into the house. Emptying the bag onto the breakfast bar we started to look through the contents.

There was just over a couple of bucks in coins, a few receipts from the liquor store and a piece of paper, folded, that contained the office address. Flicking through the note pad however, was interesting. Padriac had made a list. He had the address of the office, the house, even details of the car and its license plate. Underlined were two words, Guiseppi Morietti. He had made the connection between Travis and Joe. It wasn’t a secret that we had known Joe. Many people would have, and it was still the case that some would spend a few minutes sharing their memories of him with us. However, these people were locals, older people that remembered, not someone from New York.

“So he knew something,” Travis said.

“Seems that way.”

“Fucking shame we didn’t sober him up and ask.”

“Not worth it, bro. He’s out of the way now, that’s all that matters,” I said.

It had crossed my mind, the previous day, to find out exactly what he knew but the outcome would have been the same. I didn’t want for Travis to hear anything that came out of Padriac’s mouth. Although it was interesting to know Padriac had found out addresses and car details, there was very little else written down. Knowing how dumb it was for even that small amount of information to be recorded, I believed, whatever he knew, it would have been in that note book. We took all the papers, the note book and placed them in the hearth, setting fire to them and watching until there was nothing left but a small pile of ash.

Travis left and I headed for the shower. I closed my eyes and let the water run over my face, tilting it towards the shower head. I tried to conjure up some feeling towards what we had done, but nothing came. Was I so heartless that I couldn't feel even the slightest remorse? Even killing a man for justifiable reasons deserved some feeling. There was no doubt Padriac was a threat to me and my family and that threat had to be dealt with. He couldn't be allowed to blackmail or talk, but what was more important, he had beaten and abused my brother. I wouldn't allow anyone to hurt my family and live after.

Chapter Eight

The following morning it was business as usual. Travis had the car ready and this time, as I left the house I was greeted with a smile.

“Morning bro,” he said.

“You sleep okay?” I asked.

“Best night’s sleep I’ve had in ages.”

We stood and looked at each other, only for a few seconds, smiled and gave each other a nod. No words were needed. I was going into battle again, this time in a perfectly legal sense. An all day meeting was scheduled to bash out the details of what was proving to be a difficult takeover. A failing company, one that had also defaulted on its loan repayment to Vassago but it had good premises and it was being fought over. I wanted it, another company also wanted it.

I took my seat in the boardroom before the other parties arrived, sipping on the strong coffee Gina had placed in front of me. One by one my team filed in, Jonathan and our three lawyers. We sat and waited. Twenty minutes after the meeting was scheduled to start I heard talking and laughter from outside. Three gentlemen were shown in to a room of silent anger. They must have picked up on the atmosphere, their laughter died down and they quickly took their seats. I hadn’t risen nor offered my hand.

“We thought we would start the meeting with the concerns from the shareholders,” I was told.

I looked coldly at the young man sitting across from me. For a few seconds there was silence in the room, other than the shifting of bodies on chairs as they grew more uncomfortable under my stare.

"You can start the meeting by apologising for being late and I don't give a fuck about the concerns from the shareholders," I said.

Jonathan coughed to conceal his chuckle.

"I, err, right. First, may I apologise for our lateness, we were caught in traffic," came the reply.

"And you don't have a cell?" I asked.

"Well, yes, I should have called, I'm sorry."

Now the meeting would start just the way I wanted, with the other party on the back foot, already intimidated. I was annoyed at their lateness, not as much as I pretended to be but it was as good a reason as any to gain the upper hand.

"Before we start, your shareholders need to understand one thing. If they had done their job, if they had shown the same concern over their failing business as they are showing now, we might not be sitting here. So as far as their concerns go, I'm not interested. They either pay me my money, which we all know they can't do, or they bail out and I take the business. I'm not a charity, gentlemen. I've been patient, I've been fobbed off and promises have been broken. We are not here to negotiate, we are here to settle this," I said.

I then rested back in my chair, leaving the lawyers to do their bit.

****

It had been a stressful day and as I crossed the foyer to leave the office by the parking lot door, something made me stop. A sensation in my stomach pulled me up short. I looked around and saw a woman with black hair enter the building. She held a piece of paper in her hand. I stood and watched when her step faltered, her head dip slightly as if she had heard or felt something and she glanced around. She couldn't have seen me, I was standing against the wall just out of her view, but something had disturbed her that much was clear. She approached the security desk in the foyer asking for directions. There was something about her, even from a distance that drew me to her, that made me want to know more. I didn't fully understand but she was like a magnet, pulling me. I told Travis to wait in the car and I made my way over to the desk after she had left.

"Stan, where was that young woman off to?" I asked.

"Good Evening, Mr. Stone," he said. "She's a friend of Sam Crawley, he rang down for me to look out for her. I sent her up to the tenth floor, I hope that was okay, Sir?"

"Of course, Stan," I replied as I made my way over to the closing elevator.

I caught the next one and exited on the same floor. Sam, I noticed, was busy on the phone and I watched as she made her way to the kitchen, I followed. As I entered, I saw that she had her back to me but her body stilled, tensed. She knew I was behind her yet I had been so silent she couldn't have heard me. I saw her hands grip the counter top as she slowly turned to face me.

I found myself looking into the deepest blue eyes I'd ever seen. Against the black of her hair and the paleness of her skin, her eyes resembled the colour of the deepest oceans. She looked straight back at me, her eyes locked on mine. She didn't speak and neither did I. Truthfully, I was lost for words. For the first time in my life, I couldn't utter a sound. I saw something flash in her eyes, she frowned slightly and all the time I felt an utter compulsion to move closer to her. I watched her lips part slightly as if she was about to speak and all I could think about was that I wanted to cover those lips with mine. I wanted to kiss her, desperately, and I never kissed anyone. I wanted my tongue to dip into her mouth, to taste her. I wanted to inhale her scent. I wanted to feel her skin and the curves of her body.

I watched as she took a deep breath, perhaps to calm herself. Her features had softened, no longer was she anxious and the corners of her mouth twitched slightly, a smile starting to form. I saw her eyes look over my shoulder to the sound of the kitchen door opening. Sam had obviously finished his call. It annoyed me that the moment had been broken, yet it was an opportunity to find out who she was.

"Oh, good evening, Mr. Stone. I didn't realise you were working late," Sam stammered.

"Always, Sam. Now, introduce me to your friend," I asked.

My voice was low, even to my ears. It was an effort to speak normally, to conceal the longing I felt. Sam told me her name, Brooke Stiles, and that she was from the UK. I reached out with my hand and as I closed it around hers I saw her eyes widen a little. What disturbed me was the current I felt shoot up my arm and explode in my brain.

"Pleased to meet you, Miss Stiles. I look forward to seeing more of you," I said, cringing inside at how corny that sounded.

Finally she spoke and I was mesmerised by her soft accent.

"Umm, pleased to meet you too, Mr. Stone," she said.

I opened my hand to pull away and as I did, her fingers trailed across my palm as if not wanting the contact to end and leaving a tingling.

I wanted to stay, I wanted Sam to leave and to be able to stare into her eyes for a little while longer but I also needed to go. Something was happening to me, something I didn't understand. My brain was foggy, my stomach had a knot and I felt this pull towards her. It was as if my body took on a will of its own. I had no control and the one thing I never liked was losing control. I spun on my heels and walked away.

Every step away from her I took, that pull I felt got stronger, urging me to turn back. I fought it, hating it for taking over my body. Now irritated, I jabbed my finger on the call button waiting impatiently for the elevator doors to open. Why I was irritated, I didn't know. All I was sure of was that there was something very special about that woman.

I entered the elevator and as the doors started to close I saw Brooke and Sam leave the kitchen and walk towards me. I watched her eyes lock on mine again and I held her stare until the doors finally closed. Releasing a breath I hadn't realised I had held, I leaned against the wall, letting my head fall back and closed my eyes. She was imprinted behind my eyelids. It was those eyes that captivated me the most. There was such knowing in them. Her soft, slightly plump lips that I wanted to take between my teeth, came a close second.

And then it dawned on me. I wanted her, badly. Not to fuck, I wanted to know her, mind, body and soul. I opened my eyes and banged my fists against the steel wall as the elevator made its way slowly to the parking lot. What the fuck was happening to me? Her name rolled off my tongue, involuntarily, and I took a sharp breath in. I needed to get a grip, and quickly.

The doors opened and I made my way to the car, I spotted Travis leaning against the Range Rover.

"You okay, bro?" He asked, concern etched on his face.

"Sure, let's get out of here," I replied.

I was silent on the journey home, my face turned to the side window watching the world go by. Occasionally I would catch Travis glance in the rear view mirror, his forehead furrowed with worry. We pulled onto the drive at home and I opened the car door.

"Rob, you sure you're okay? You seem quiet," he asked again.

"Sure, Trav. Sorry, just got something on my mind, that's all. I'll see you in the morning," I replied, making it clear I didn't want company.

As I climbed the stairs to the lounge, I smelt food. I wasn't hungry but Evelyn had prepared a pasta dish for me. I should have texted and told her not to bother but I felt bad enough not talking to Travis. I dished up a small plate while she asked me about my day.

"Busy, I feel shattered. Think I'm going to have an early night," I said, probably not that convincingly. But somehow I couldn't stop a stupid grin from spreading across my face.

She looked at me, her forehead furrowed.

"Whatever has you busy, shattered, seems to have put a smile on your face. A smile, I might add, that I haven't seen in ages," she said.

"Okay, something happened today, something I don't quite understand."

"Want to talk about it?"

"I'm not sure what it is, I just know I've found her."

When the words left my mouth I realised I should have kept quiet. Evelyn was looking at me as if I had just lost it. The strange thing was, as much as I had no idea why I had said those words, on an emotional level I couldn't get to, I knew I would, at some point, understand. I'd found her. I didn't know who she was, I knew nothing about her yet I knew she was going to be important to me.

"Do you want to talk about it?" Evelyn asked.

"No because I don't understand what this means but I've met someone. Someone I think is going to be important to me. I'm sorry, Ev, I'm just tired I guess. My head feels like it's about to explode right now."

"Okay, you rest up and I'll see you tomorrow," she replied as she made her way to the stairs.

With the house empty I finally relaxed, pouring myself a glass of wine and sitting on the sofa. I tried to empty my mind of the image of Brooke, empty my senses of her smell, of the feel of her fingers trailing across my palm, to no avail. I ran my hand through my hair. Finally I headed downstairs. I showered, standing under the jets until the water scolded my skin, dried myself and climbed into bed. The oddest thing happened. I slid my hand across the cool cotton sheets over to one side, as if I was reaching out for someone. I wondered what it would feel like to have her in my bed, in my home, somewhere I had never brought anyone before. I screwed my eyes shut, I was definitely losing it. I shook my head and laughed.

It was in that small room in my office block in Washington, DC, that my life changed, forever.

Dear Reader,

So now you know. This is me, the good and the bad. I haven't told you my story as eloquently as perhaps I should have. I still find it hard to express my feelings, to know the right words even.

Am I a product of my upbringing? Probably. But I have also chosen to live the life I have. I have done terrible things and I've survived terrible things. I am a wealthy man because of it. Would I change my life? No, I wouldn't change one day. I suffered, I was abused, beaten, I've been hungry, cold and lost. Yet all of that has shaped me into the man I am today.

There are thoughts and feelings swimming around in my head and my body that I don't understand. I do know I have met a remarkable woman, one who is going to be vital to my existence. One that is going to totally own me, screw with my head until I either explode or give in to her. All I hope is that my fight instinct doesn't last long. I want to give in to her, I need her and I don't know why. And as for this feeling of having found her. I have no idea what that means. The only way I can describe it is, have you ever meet someone and within a couple of minutes you feel you have known them for a lifetime? The connection you have with them is that strong. That feeling is coursing through my body and to have that must mean I met her before, doesn't it?

In those few moments, in that kitchen, I felt the strangest, the calmest, the most emotional and scared I had ever felt. Confused? So am I.

Brooke Stiles means something more than just a friend of an employee, I know that. What she means, I have a feeling I'm about to find out. And you know what? I have no doubt this isn't going to be easy. But I have the strangest understanding that she is going to be worth the trauma I'm about to go through. All I can hope is that she is strong enough to stay with me while I fight through that and she is strong enough to accept who I really am.

Robert Stone

Made in the USA
Charleston, SC
25 February 2015